# I F-ING DARE YOU

*All The Games We Play Book One*

MAY SAGE

I Fucking Dare You

All The Games We Play # 1

By Emm Darcy | May Sage



Edited by Theresa Schultz and Nicole Zoltak

Proofread by Sue Currin

Paperback Cover Art by Sweet 'N Spicy Designs

❀ Created with Vellum

# PROLOGUE

I should look away. I should walk away. I don't, because I can't. My feet are firmly planted on the polished floor; they might as well be encased in concrete. The writhing bodies have me entranced, their song and sinful dance, enraptured.

I'm not shocked. Shock would imply a degree of surprise. There's nothing surprising in finding the four of them in the locker room—the girls', too—with a girl. They're fucking. There's no other word for it. They aren't making love, they certainly aren't sleeping with her. They're fucking her. Hard. I can't even see her face, just her long, dark locks. There are hundreds of dark-haired girls in Cross and Roses. I couldn't begin to guess which one these boys have chosen for their depravity. Every girl wants at least one of them, if not the four of them together. She could have been me, for all intents and purposes. Not that I'd ever even dreamt of any of them fucking me. I don't exist. Not to them—not to most people in this joke of a school.

*Get out of here,* I tell myself, all the while leaning forward to get a better view of Jason's face.

The latest survey on SnapApp showed that the girls (and boys—though many wouldn't admit to voting) of Cross think that Maverick is the prettiest of the four. I can see it. Both of his parents are mixed race; he took away the best of all ethnicities. His caramel skin and long dark lashes clash with his emerald green eyes. I can't see him from this angle. Just his cock. The girl's seated on his lap, bouncing up and down while Rowan fucks her from behind, his perfect ass diving into her with abandon.

Cain came in second on the survey; Jason was last. Maybe because he doesn't smile. Maybe because he's known to be merciless to friends and foes alike. I'll never understand my peers. All four of them may be golden Greek gods among mere mortals, but my eyes have always gravitated to Jason. He's fascinating. And he's never been more fascinating than right now. While Cain plunges in and out of the girl's mouth, Jason watches. Fully clothed, he stares at the girl, a hand running down the length of her dark hair. I see his mouth move, but over the moans and grunts and sweet curses, I can't hear his whispers. They're all for her. Their secret.

I've never been so hot, and cold, and terrified. What if they see me?

What if they don't?

# CHAPTER ONE

I should have worn sneakers. God knows I love my painted Docs, but they aren't much help on a three-mile trek.

*Fuck*. I can't afford to be late, not today.

I had a deal with my parents: whatever I save for my car fund, they'd match it to help me pay for my ride. I'd bought my dream car—a racing green Mini with a checkered rooftop—just two weeks ago, and it's already broken down twice. The second time was at five this morning. After desperately attempting to breathe life into it again, I had to face the music and ask Dad to drive me up to school. Except he was already at the restaurant, supervising a supply run. He came as soon as he could, but I'm still behind schedule.

It would help if parents could directly drive up to the school building, but that wasn't allowed without prior written authorization, as well as an ironclad reason. Cross and Roses took the privacy of its students fucking seriously.

I love the campus, most days. It's vast enough to walk around and forget where I am when I need an escape. The gates open to a paved road leading right up to the common dorm, a four-story building that looks more like a manor house than a place meant for teenage students. A courtyard separates the dorm from the administrative building where I still need to drop by to pick up my new assigned room number and schedule.

Past the administrative building that doubles as a residence for the staff, the campus boasts a lake, near which the legacies' dorm was built. The lake house makes the common dorm-slash-manor look like a hovel. It's a wood and glass contemporary home built less than ten years ago by a world-renowned architect who used to attend Cross. He got the multimillion-dollar contract just like that. Nepotism, anyone?

The lake house—we call it Glass—belongs to the legacies. No one can go anywhere near it without their permission, so I've never caught a glimpse from up close.

The school keeps horses near the grove. The stables overlook a field where our cross-country team likes to run. It looks nothing like a school. Our actual lessons happen one mile from the stables, in a U-shaped building modeled after the Louvre. I doubt the French palace is as gaudy as Cross, with our burgundy curtains, velvet-lined high-backed chairs, and ceilings painted with naked baby angels. Not that I'd know—unlike most of the student body, I've never been to France.

At least no one has dropped a pyramid in the middle of the courtyard. Yet.

Dad had to drop me off at the gates, so I walked all the way up to the school building. At the top of each hour, buses run between the dorm and the school, but I was far too late to catch one.

I scan my student card and rush into the amphitheater where assemblies are held each week. Relief crashes into my chest when I see it hasn't started yet. Being late to any assembly was worth a detention and a demerit—enough demerits could lead to a suspension. I can't afford any of that nonsense on my transcript. I hurry to claim the first open seat I spy, toward the back.

Moments after I take my seat, our severe headmaster, Mr. Bone, marches to the platform, and the crowd silences without him having to say a single word. He launches into the usual boring lecture, addressing each class with gravitas that doesn't quite hit after the first time. The freshmen are warned that their decisions will determine their entire future, and they look downright terrified at the prospect—like I had been two years ago. To us, he drones on about our final year being the most important one. "You need to focus on looking good for your college applications."

Seriously? Who would've thought that? I roll

my eyes. I'm tired of older people assuming that because we're young, we must be completely dumb.

Between waiting tables, I'd had summer classes at Tisch, and more than ever, I want to get in. With hard work, determination, and a lack of distractions, I should be able to. I may not be the best in math and science, but I'll work as hard as I can to show them I'm worth taking a chance on. The light at the end of the tunnel makes the pain worth it. I'll go to Tisch, learn multiple mediums, make connections in the art world, and hopefully, someday sell a painting or two.

I'm not deluded. I realize that I'm likely to become a high school art teacher to pay the bills—or college, if I'm lucky. But I would do my damnedest to ingest art every day. I don't want to end up working behind a desk at a nine-to-five job like my father did before he started the restaurant. He hated it, and I'd hate it more. His first love is cooking. Mine is creating.

There's some laughter and a few whispers behind me, and I glance over my shoulder.

It's *them*.

Of course it is.

Heat rushes up my neck and to my cheeks like it has every time I've thought about them this summer.

I didn't constantly waste my time daydreaming about boys who had no idea who I was of course, but memories of that day at the end of last year have popped up inadvertently now and then. Especially at night.

Summer has been good to them. They've always been athletic, as they play football, but they've filled out, looking more like men than boys these days. Just as delicious, a little more dangerous.

The legacies might run this school, but Cain, Maverick, Rowan, and Jason run the legacies. In a world where money and connections are the most important things, they hail from the richest families.

I don't envy most of my peers. I don't wish I had their money or their connections. Those four, I'm insanely jealous of. Their confidence is staggering. If I could bottle it and sell it, I'd be as rich as any of them.

They're just five seats away from me. I look away, staring at the headmaster. At least any bystander would have thought I was. From the corner of my eyes, I ogled. I ogled hard.

The four kings are thoroughly ignoring our headmaster, entertaining themselves. A couple of girls giggle at whatever joke they started. I shake my head. It's not like they're dumb either. They just know that his speech isn't for them. Whatever they do, they'll land in a cushy job that leaves plenty of time for their hobbies, their mistresses, weekly golf, and regular beach holidays.

Lucky assholes. They don't mind being spotted disrupting the assembly because Mr. Bone is, for all intents and purposes, their employee. I wish I could do just about anything other than wasting an hour listening to drivel, but Mr. Bone's approval is a necessity to me. My entire transcript needs to sparkle so hard it looks like a unicorn farted all over it.

It would be nice to just have fun. Maybe in another life.

I redirect my eyes firmly toward the front of the room and listen to the rest of the lecture in silence.

# CHAPTER TWO

Half running to catch the bus, I pull my phone out of my blazer, unsurprised to find a series of texts on my screen.

**Where are you??**

**So help me god, if you're not coming this year and you didn't tell me...**

**Did you get kidnapped?**

**Tell me you're not in a ditch somewhere.**

**WHERE ARE YOU???!?**

My best friend has no chill. Never one to be late to anything, Sophia seldom fails to panic when I don't show up where I'm supposed to, when I'm supposed to. Which admittedly is often.

I shoot her a quick answer, still jogging through the familiar corridors. I'll be late to my first class, but it beats showing up late to the assembly. Mr. Bone has a stick up his ass and warped notions of his self-importance. Most teachers can be reasoned with.

Cross and Roses is one of the world's most coveted boarding schools. Uncle Lucius enrolled my cousin Lucas in ninth grade to get him away from the influence of some of his junior high friends in the city. Impressed by the school, he'd offered to pay for my tuition starting my sophomore year.

The modern campus is tucked away in upstate New York, protected by high walls and higher entry requirements. This is a prep school reserved for the ultra-rich or the ultra-talented. I'm not either, but when Uncle Lucius suggested enrolling me, I jumped into his arms and begged my parents to accept his generosity. Graduating from here is the one highlight of my otherwise average transcript. I know it will change my life for the better.

I'm proud of my father's achievement. His dad, my grandfather, who died before I was born, immigrated from Italy, and became a cliche: his family ran a criminal group doing god knows what. Dad and Uncle Lucius both walked away from organized crime. All that matters to my father is sharing his Nonna's recipes with the world. Uncle Lucius is more ambitious; he opened a now-successful PR company in the city.

They're both remarkable in their own ways, but I don't want to walk in either of their footsteps. I like cooking well enough, but it's not my vocation. PR sounds like a bore to me. I have to make my own mark in the world, cultivating my own passions. And that means going to college. This school is just a pit stop. My application to Tisch is going to be well-padded, thanks to the school's reputation. My advisor has been helpful from the moment I told him I wanted in to the art school.

This is my third year here; I know the corridors well enough to take a few shortcuts on my way to the entrance.

I'm approaching the entrance of the underground state-of-the-art gym when a commotion begins prickling my ears. I'm late enough as it is, I should just be on my way, but something bothers me.

There are half-whispers and sharp noises—like someone kicking a metal locker, maybe.

A girl whimpers. "I promise, it wasn't me. I wouldn't do that. You know me."

I still at the top of the stairs. I know that voice.

"Oh, yes, Jude. We know you, all right." This is delivered with venom and accompanied with another shove of metal.

I'm late already, but this is important. Bullying is a major problem here. The entitled pricks of this school think they can get away with murder and most of the time, they're right. I'm not relevant enough for anyone to have attacked me yet, but it could be me down there, getting shoved by some guy. I have to do *something*.

Spotting the phone still in my hand, I load my camera app. The school closes their eyes to most shenanigans so long as money keeps rolling in, but when there's tangible proof, they're obliged to act, if only to preserve their reputation.

It's not my business, but as far as I'm concerned, knowing indifference is just as bad as bullying. Resolved, I walk down the stairs, holding the phone up high.

Jason, Cain, Rowan, and Maverick corner Judith Cushman.

*Fuck.*

The situation couldn't be any worse.

Judith's a friend. Sort of. We were assigned as lab partners last year. A chatterbox with an easy smile and an easier laugh, she didn't sign up for the elitist bullshit everyone else seems to drink for breakfast. Besides, she's the reason I ended up with straight As in science for the first time in my life.

My stomach churns. As I approach the group, I can barely make out Rowan's words, but I hear enough that it sounds threatening. It looks threatening, too, as he leans forward, caging Judith in with his arms. She presses against the lockers, her expression twisted in fear as she shakes her head, as if willing her reality away. Her short bob fans out from around her face, the blonde strands covering her mouth.

My hand steadily holds the phone, capturing every moment of this. I can't deny I'm surprised.

They might rule this place, but those four aren't the kind to get their hands dirty. I've never seen them trip, insult, or throw slurs at anyone. Why are they doing this? What is it all about?

And Judith is one of them, a legacy. She lives in Glass, and her parents are all members of the esteemed Heritage Club in the city. I'm not involved with any of the cliques here, but I still know what goes on around most of the school. I hadn't thought there were many secrets, because gossip runs rampant, but there's definitely something going on here.

I glance up and down the stairs. No one else is around. They clearly picked this spot intentionally for...for whatever this is.

My eyes seek out Jason. I always see Jason first. He's leaning back against the opposite wall like a king overseeing his knights' work. His tousled blond hair contrasts with the darkness of his gray eyes, sharp as the edge of a knife. His lips are full, and when he licks them, I want to look away. I don't. I need to take all of this in, if only to end my fascination with him right here and now. He's clearly an asshole.

Rowan's done, but now Cain's talking to Judith. His voice is a little louder.

"Jude, Jude, Jude. You know better than to mess up in M.E. You're going to have to pay. I don't care if you have to spread your legs to every cock in the club next time."

Her eyes widen; she's even more terrified. "Please, Cain."

There is no pity in his dark eyes. Cain Warren is supposed to be a tech genius—he's already launched apps that presumably made him rich in his own right—but if that doesn't work out for him and the endless pool of money his family swims in runs out, he could make a career out of his pretty face one way or another. Before today, I would have paid good money to see him on the big screen. Just him, preferably shirtless. He doesn't even have to say anything. His brown wavy hair always falls forward across his forehead, just begging to be brushed back.

Now, all pretense of civilization has been stripped. He's a brute.

Rowan smiles like the whole scene amuses him. Bastard.

Maverick, at least, seems to hesitate. "We get it. You were having a little too much fun. It didn't hit you at the time that you might have crossed a line." His fist moves to rest on the locker right next to her head. "But you did. It's going to cost us, which means that it'll cost *you*."

"I'm sorry, please..."

Something inside me snaps, and before I can stop myself, I walk forward, quickly closing the distance between us.

"Leave her alone," I demand, my voice not shaking one bit, even though my knees are. I hold my phone up to Maverick's face. "I got all that on camera. Oh, and my shit uploads online instantly, so you can't take the phone. Let her go right now or it's going straight to Mr. Bone."

# CHAPTER THREE

My courageous little speech sounded like a good idea in my head. As their four pairs of eyes—as well as Judith's stunned gaze—turn to me, my small phone feels like a paper shield, only useful in make-believe fights against the imaginary dragons in my head. Those four boys are real, and really fucking pissed.

I stand there like a moron, shocked at my own audacity. Judith's frozen, like me. We're both prey among predators. I don't know what they're going to do next, but I don't want to be there for it.

I take a step back, still clinging to my bravado, before it leaves my system. "Let her go, don't bother her again, and I'll delete the video. Otherwise, I'll send it." The word vomit won't stop coming out of my mouth, although I'm starting to get the feeling that I'm making things worse and worse for myself.

Repeating my threat, I walk back to the stairs,

forcing myself not to run. Like I need to look any more like prey.

Finally, Cain laughs. Rowan and Maverick do the same, but Jason? He continues to stare at me, unreadable.

Judith is the first to speak. "Nadia, it's all right." She attempts the most pitiful semblance of a smile. "Nothing's going on. You can go."

I gape at her, so confused that I'm rendered mute. She's...taking their side?

"It's not what it looks like," she adds.

My cheeks feel so hot. "No?" I press, a frown between my brows. "Because it looks like you're getting bullied."

Jason smiles.

I've never seen him smile. Not once. Not with his friends, when everyone else is laughing. Not at any of the girls practically throwing themselves at him. It's both beautiful and horrifying. It's a cruel smile that doesn't reach the depths of his icy gray eyes. He looks like he's about to enjoy ripping the wings off a butterfly.

Unfortunately, the butterfly is likely to be me.

"I don't think you understand that word, cupcake," he tells me, though Judith just said my name. He approaches me slowly. I try to walk back again, but my foot hits the stairs, and he reaches me before I can flee. When he bends to reach my ear, I catch a whiff of seaside and wind, a fresh smell, subtle and unique. "You will."

He walks up the stairs, hands in his pocket, positively nonchalant. As if he hasn't just threatened two girls in the hallway.

Maverick elbows Rowan, who brushes back his long hair—not that it ever bothers to stay back. "This is interesting."

"You think?" the blond giant shoots back.

They're enjoying themselves. That's plain to see. They feed off my fear, and I can't truly hide it.

I notice Cain when he calls me, echoing Jason. "Cupcake? You might want to have that phone checked out." The asshole winks, holding his own phone up.

I glance down at my black screen. I try to activate the screen, again and again, and to reboot it, all in vain.

*Shit*!

I hadn't even noticed him doing anything, but somehow, with nothing other than his own cell phone, he's destroyed mine.

The other three boys follow Jason, thoroughly entertained. I watch them leave, unmoving, my heart beating too fast in my chest.

*Holy shit. So, that just happened.*

It feels like an end. A beginning. The kind of choice that's going to matter to my future—like having braces or cutting my hair in seventh grade, only much bigger. A choice I'm going to regret. They'll make sure I do.

Once they've disappeared from view, Judith

clears her throat. "Thank you," she says, holding my eyes so I can see she's sincere. "You're worried for nothing, though. I wasn't getting...bullied." She winced as she said the word, like voicing it might make it real. "I just made the wrong choices at their club, and I'm paying for it."

"Their club?" I'm confused.

Judith hooks her arm through mine and starts to walk up the stairs. "They own a club in the city together." She shrugs like it's no big deal. I suppose to her, it isn't. "It's a tradition for legacy kids to get a lump sum when we turn eighteen. It comes directly from our parents' club, if we join it."

I've always known they lived in a different world, but what the fuck?

"Cain was born in February, Rowan in April, Maverick and Jason around May, so they all got theirs last year. They pooled it together to buy a failing club in the city at the beginning of the summer. It's already the hottest new place. I went this weekend, and well..."

Judith lowers her gaze. She's picking at her nails. I doubt it's a habit; they're perfect, like the rest of her. Her head snaps up, and she meets my gaze. "I bought some weed there," she admits. "But the police raided the place this weekend, and the club got a big fine. The guys wanted to know who I'd bought it from, and well, I don't want a drug dealer on my ass, so I kept my mouth shut. They aren't happy about that."

I swallow hard. Great. I'm *so* glad I opened up

my big trap. I don't judge easily; a few of the girls I wait tables with at my dad's restaurant smoke. It's legal in New York, who cares? But they're over twenty-one. If Judith chooses to take drugs underage, well, it's not exactly my business, is it?

I stepped into a mess that I had no business stepping in.

I can understand both sides of it—if it had happened in my dad's restaurant, he would also have wanted to know the identity of the drug dealer selling to minors on his turf to stop that nonsense. And I'm not dumb enough to fail to see why Judith would stay silent to protect herself.

Bottom line, she fucked up and has to deal with the consequences. I drink from time to time at parties with a fake ID. If I got caught, I'd expect to have to clean up a mess, too, though perhaps not a mess as terrifying as the four idols of Cross.

It's time for me to back down and keep my head buried in the sand.

If it isn't too late already.

*You will.*

Jason's warning replays at the back of my mind.

Maybe I can talk to him. Let him know I've deleted the video. He'd leave me alone then, right?

"If you're sure you're alright," I murmur.

"You're sweet, Nadia, but like I said, I'm fine. I grew up with those four, you know?" Judith smiles widely. "They might act like brutes from time to time, but they'll never hurt me."

True enough.

Hurting me is another matter.

"You think we'll have science together again?"

The reminder that I don't have my schedule although class started over fifteen minutes ago, makes me leap into action. "Shit! I need to go to the admin building. Catch you later?"

# CHAPTER FOUR

I take the bus back. First thing in the morning and at three when school lets out, about ten buses run between the school and the dorm, but there's a shuttle service running every half hour. I'm going to be so late to the first class, a few more minutes won't hurt. My teacher's likely to be more charitable than the headmaster would have been if I'd missed his rubbish assembly.

I'm alone on the bus, and the driver, Ivan, chats merrily about his summer, not discouraged by my monosyllabic answers. My mind's still on the incident earlier. What are the chances of the four kings of this school giving me a pass? None, that's what. I shoved my foot where it didn't belong and I know there will be consequences unless I can defuse the situation.

I'm going to need to apologize. Part of me recoils at the idea. They *were* being asses. Who cares what she did—it wasn't okay for four men built like tanks to intimidate one girl like that, in a dark corner.

When Ivan drops me off, I cross the courtyard and make my way through the lobby, inside Ms. Casey's office. The admin assistant smiles kindly, showing perfectly straight pearly whites. "Nadia. Welcome back."

I'm impressed that she remembers my name. I don't often pop by the administrative building. "Thank you, Ms. Casey. I hope you had a great summer." My customer service persona kicks in when I'm dealing with people I might eventually want something from. "I was running late this morning—car trouble."

Her eyes widen. I suppose that's one excuse she doesn't hear often around here. My fellow students mostly drive brand-new cars that cost the price of a reasonably situated two-bedroom apartment; their cars didn't break down.

She recovers quickly and shuffles through her desk. "I wondered why you hadn't come to pick up your details." Having found what she was looking for, Ms. Casey hands me a leather-covered handbook with my name stamped in gold foil.

This school is ridiculous.

"There's been an update to the school rules. We wouldn't want last winter's incident to happen again."

I nod sagely, like I remember whatever she's talking about. "Who'd want that?" It's also fairly possible that no one thought to gossip with me about it at the time.

My cheeks heat, unbidden.

Suddenly I can remember one specific incident from last summer, right before school break. Four guys, one dark-haired girl between them. The memory often rises to the surface without my say-so.

My mind races, and I imagine the anonymous brunette being cornered and threatened too. Maybe it was their MO. Maybe that girl had been forced to do *that* with all of them because she'd crossed some arbitrary line with those self-centered pricks.

But I remember her moans, her pleas for more. At the time, I never would have thought that she could be screwing them for any other reason than her own pleasure. After this morning, my view of those guys has shifted.

They're dangerous.

How dangerous, I'll never find out.

"I see you've requested to drop the track team?" She brings me back to reality.

I nod, forcing the porn replaying in my brain out of my mind.

I like running well enough, but seniors take the sport seriously and that's not my focus. "Is that a problem?"

"Not necessarily, but you'll want your schedule as attractive as possible." She doesn't say the obvious: unlike most students here, I can't rely on my parents' wallet to open doors with a mediocre transcript. She might have had a point if I was interested in Harvard or Yale, but I'd like to think Tisch pays more attention to artistic abilities.

"I still have swimming," I point out.

There were two swimming teams in Cross. Our varsity team does pretty well when we compete, and that makes them far too serious about it for my liking. I tried it in sophomore year, mostly to spend time with Sophia, but I don't have a competitive nature; not when it comes to sports, in any case. I joined the regular swim team.

"I see." She didn't have to say much, her expression made it clear she didn't think colleges would consider that enough. "Well, I suggest you discuss your schedule with the school advisor after school today, if you'd like to talk it through."

I don't, but her clear disapproval makes me doubt my decisions. I figured focusing on art made sense, but what if she is right?

"We may not be able to change your classes after this week. But with advance placements in English and art, you have plenty to do already." She prints my schedule and hands it to me. "You're on the top floor. Single room."

"Really?" I try not to groan.

Ms. Casey beams at me, like she's delivering good news. There's only one floor with single rooms—enough for about half the senior class—and those rooms are prized. In truth, I would have much preferred to room with Sophia.

"Thanks."

"You're going to need a pass." Ms. Casey glances at the big grandfather clock in her otherwise modern office. "Actually, it looks like you'll be missing first period completely. I'll send a message to your teacher. Head over to your second period now, and try not to be late again this week."

I nod and thank her again. Other than for assemblies, this school is generally pretty chill about the occasional tardy.

I get out of the room, still a little disappointed, and also confused. It is peculiar that I was allotted a single room when I didn't even request one. Usually, the prerogative goes to students whose parents donate a hefty amount to the library or the stables. Maybe I'm the token poor kid on the upper floor, to pretend that favoritism doesn't come into play with room assignments. It's still strange that it was given to *me*, when I asked to share.

I suppose Sophia might have requested to be alone this year. We never talked about it. We were assigned together randomly in sophomore year and became fast friends. The two subsequent years, she and I asked to share a room again. I simply assumed we would do the same our senior year, but she might have had other plans.

It'd be fine. It'd be like home again. Besides, Sophia was terribly untidy. Still, it felt like losing a security blanket.

I wait a few minutes for the bus, checking my phone, hoping to catch up on the notification on SnapApp.

My phone takes a while to turn on; at first, I don't think it will at all, but when it does, my jaw falls open. It's empty, completely wiped clean. There's no picture, no apps—everything is gone, even my screensaver.

Cain. He's somehow managed to do that to my phone from his. I have to reset my credentials everywhere. Thankfully, I only use three variations of the same password. It's easy enough to get it back up and running.

To satisfy paranoid parents, the school pays for a private server for the student body—we need a student ID to sign in, although they say our communications aren't monitored. I don't believe a word of it; I'd never post anything here that I wouldn't be comfortable telling a teacher, so my own feed is basically empty. Still, it helps me stay in touch with what's going on at Cross.

The bulk of my peers have no problem plastering their lives on our private social media. I see shots of their holidays, their new cars, Louboutin pumps, and more.

I suppose nothing much has happened so far. Last year, it was full of half-naked shots under the bleachers, or blurry pictures of girls straddling faceless guys. The bus arrives, and I pocket my phone, bracing myself.

Time to return to reality.

A reality where I've royally pissed off the four kings of this place. And I'm about to walk back into the lion's den.

# CHAPTER FIVE

I take a moment to study my schedule on the steps in front of the U. It looks like I missed calculus. I wince. What sort of sadist would set up calculus for first period? Next, I have Italian, then two hours of AP literature, so the morning improves at least. Lunch is at twelve thirty, followed by gym, a free period, and AP art. The regular swim team meets from five thirty to six thirty. Dinner is served from six thirty to eight, and for seniors, there is a strict curfew at ten thirty. We'd gained half an hour since last year.

That meant I was free from six-thirty to ten. Homework would kick my ass senior year, of course, but maybe Ms. Casey had a point; I could shoulder another elective that made my transcript stronger, so long as the timing worked out.

The first bell rings and I make my way to Italian, absentmindedly scrolling through the school website to see if there's something suitable in my free period, when abruptly, someone throws their arms around me. I grin, already knowing who it is. My list of friends is short, and only one of them smells like vanilla cupcake.

Sure enough, I glance over my shoulder to see Sophia Vaughn. "See? I'm still alive."

"Alive and late." She couldn't sound more judgmental if she tried. "On our first day."

"Car troubles," I sum up.

"Again?" She winces. "You got swindled with that car."

I refuse to acknowledge that. She might have a point, but dammit, I'm going to enjoy the fact that I *have* a car, at least. She doesn't get it because her parents had a pink Jeep under a big red bow at her sweet sixteen—brand new, of course. I never would have dared to ask for a car. Dad's always worried about bills, especially after the various lockdowns in the last few years. Mom's a spender; she wears a new pair of shoes or handbag every month, which is just rude when he stays up until two in the morning most nights to provide for us. I know Mom has her own money from her former career, but I don't let her spend too much of it on me. I used to think that if she wanted to dip into her savings, she can do it to pay the damn mortgage.

Mom came to me with an offer at the beginning of the summer: she'd double whatever I could save for my car. I refused initially, because I felt terrible about spending money we might need to keep a roof over our heads. When I implied as much, she laughed. "Honey, if Sandro let me, I would have paid off the townhouse ages ago. You know Astrella men—all pride, little sense. Let me do this for you, yes? So you can pick something that runs."

Paid off the house? I have no clue how much Mom has, but I wouldn't have guessed that much, though I suppose she did quite well. A ballet dancer, she toured the world for years before getting pregnant with me and setting her career aside. She teaches lessons at a local ballet school in Brooklyn now.

I accepted the deal, though her plan turned out to be a bit of a fail. Hulk—as I called my Mini—was a disaster. Even I knew that if a car broke down twice in two weeks, it sucked.

As I daydream about Hulk, wondering when Mom and Dad can finally drive it up to me, Sophia yanks my crumpled schedule out of my hand and skims it.

Her face falls, and she groans.

"That look doesn't exactly inspire confidence," I remark, wincing. "What's the damage?"

As I wait for the verdict, I take her in.

I've seen her twice this summer for coffee. Between my work and her travels, we can rarely catch up during the vacations.

Sophia's a year younger than me, but she doesn't look it. Back when we met in sophomore year, she'd had generous DDs, when I could still have worn a training bra. Two years later, she's a curvaceous bombshell, not that anyone except me seems to realize it. She isn't comfortable in her skin, so her clothes are a fair bit baggier than they need to be, drowning her frame. As much as I keep trying to convince her that she needs to flaunt her hell of a rack, she never listens to me. Her hair is gorgeous, too—dark and wavy. She tanned this summer, and the glow makes her more beautiful than ever. I wish she could see herself the way I do.

Though I suppose she'd say the same thing about me. She's all compliments, when as far as I can see, there's nothing special about my brownish hair, my brownish eyes—though they do occasionally feel like turning green—and no amount of pasta or doughnuts has helped soften my frame. I'm cute, at best, more a girl than a woman. I look like my mother in her old pictures, so I might turn out to be pretty as I age, but for now, I'm just an awkward tomboy.

"One class. That's it." She shoves my schedule back in my hand, as if the slip of paper burned her.

*Shit*. That's worse than the rooming issue.

As annoyed as I am about that—because who doesn't want every class with their closest school friend—Sophia looks downright terrified. Her lower lip is trembling and she twists her fingers nervously.

I'm not rich enough to have many friends here, but people leave me alone; I'm beneath the general notice. Sophia has a different set of problems; she's been bullied for years, mostly by her sister Brooke and Brooke's posse.

Just thinking about that bitch makes my blood

boil. I don't have a sibling, but I can't imagine treating *any* relative the way Brooke treats Sophia. The two sisters are nothing alike, inside or out. Brooke has dyed her hair blonde since she was twelve, I think, and the chemicals must've done something to her brain because the funny, sweet, intelligent genes completely skipped her. Though eighteen months apart, both of them have been in the same year as long as I've known them because Sophia skipped a grade. Which could be one of the reasons why Brooke dislikes her so much. Sophia, with her straight As, is the pride and joy of their heart-surgeon dad. Brooke, not so much.

"This year is going to suck ass," Sophia mutters.

"It'll be fine." I can't even convince myself of that; not after what happened this morning. "We'll make the most of it."

Somehow.

"You can leave campus," Sophia whines. "I'll be stuck here, and—"

"Well, I don't have a car to get out of here for now," I remind her. "But when I get Hulk back, I'll bring you iced coffees."

She manages a weak smile as the bell rings, and we have to scramble to take our seats.

Day one, we talk about the curriculum; the rest of the week, we'll be reviewing what we learned last year.

It doesn't take long for me to realize that this year is going to be challenging; we have twice the workload we did last year in Italian—one of my best subjects. The prep school isn't the best of the best just because the student body looks like models from the glossy pages of *Vogue*. It's great because our teachers are second to none. A B- from here is rated higher than an A from my old public school in Queens.

I'll forever be in Uncle Lucius's debt for being willing to foot the bill for tuition, although he won't hear of it. He's always been generous and kind to us. In many ways, I'm closer to Uncle Lucius than to my busy father. Though he ran his own company, Lucius had the time—and the extra funds—to take my cousin and me bowling or sailing on weekends. Or maybe he just *took* the time. As he often said, "family is everything" to him.

I glance over at Sophia. She's already taking notes, though Signora Di Maio is just babbling on about the upcoming spring trip, her native Italian slower so as to be understood by everyone. Mine's rusty. Dad and Uncle Lucius speak to Lucas and I in English, and Mom alternates between English and Spanish, as she's from Mexico. As a kid, our Nonna spoke to us solely in Italian. My tongue can twist over the language with some ease thanks to her, but I'm far from fluent—unlike my cousin.

Still, I'm sketching rather than paying attention. I know I won't go on the trip—it will probably cost tens of thousands, and I'm not asking Uncle Lucius. Or Dad. Or Mom.

Maybe Mom had a point about the Astrella pride. Though my surname's Reyes, as my parents weren't married yet when I was born, I have inherited my fair share of it.

Italian flies by while I'm lost in my doodles, and soon, it's time for my English class. Next is lunch. That, I'm looking forward to.

I slide into a free seat toward the middle of the class. The front is where all the brainy kids and suck-ups sit, and the back is for troublemakers and rebels. In the middle, you're overlooked, which is fine by me.

I'm already doodling, waiting for the last bell, when my fingers pause over my notebook. Feeling a gaze on me, I lift my eyes.

Jason's standing just a few feet away from me, staring silently. Cain's behind him, his smirk just as amused as it was earlier this morning.

*Oh no.*

# CHAPTER SIX

Cain chuckles. *Fuck.* I didn't mean to say that out loud. Showing weaknesses and fear to the likes of him was like bleeding in shark-infested water.

God, it's not fair how beautiful they both are. While Cain is traditionally gorgeous, to me, Jason is a lot more...interesting, I suppose. I've been fascinated since before my first day here. I met him once as a child, though I doubt he'd remember that. It was so many years ago. He'd been so cold then. A little boy with eyes as empty and calculating as any man. Part of me had found him scary. The other part doodled his eyes day after day, never quite getting them right.

The second time I set my eyes on him, he was maybe sixteen, and so much colder. The compulsion to immortalize him on paper was stronger. I even tried to sculpt him, but that had been a disaster. I'm rather tactile; to sculpt well, I need to touch my inspiration. I suppose most amateurs have that sort of crutch. I doubt he would volunteer to model for me. Still, my mind races as I imagine sculpting those hard muscles, the long lines, the sharp jawline...

*Fuck, fuck, fuck.* How did my brain even go there? I'm supposed to talk to him, apologize about earlier, not gawk at him like a future stalker.

Jason tilts his head. "Nadia, was it?"

I bite my lip. He knows my name. A few days, weeks, or years ago, that might have been exciting —though baffling. The past three years, we've never exchanged a word, or a look, or a pencil, for that matter. I didn't exist in his world before.

Right now, I do, and it's simply terrifying.

"Sorry," I blurt out.

That was the best I could do in the circumstances, with the class half-filled and almost ready to start.

The second bell rings as his tongue darts out to wet his lower lip. "You aren't. Not yet."

They both walk to their seats.

I fidget when I hear one of them drag a chair directly behind me. Cain's to my right, I can see him from the corner of my eye, which means that Jason's at my back. I fight the urge to turn around. I can't let them get to me.

A girl slides into the seat next to me, and I'm grateful for the distraction. I grin. "Melina!"

"Hey, Nadia," she says, surprising me by remembering my name. We were both on the regular swim team, but we didn't chat often. Melina's another legacy. "How was your summer?"

"Pretty good." I smile and lean closer to her, intent on putting the guys out of my mind. "I had my first tattoo done."

I seem to remember we had a conversation about body art last year. Melina said she had seven piercings and three tattoos already. I've caught a glimpse of some when she's been in her school swimsuit.

Her eyes light up. "Oooh! Can I see it?"

"Not here, it's under all this." I run my hands along the lapels of my blazer.

Black with red accents, the uniform isn't entirely terrible, especially since I dread to think how I'd stand out if we could dress as we pleased here. My wardrobe is mostly made of jeans and plain T-shirts, not designer staples.

"How about your vacation?" I finally get around to asking, but the English teacher clears his throat, and class starts.

I smile at Melina and start to sketch, forcing myself to return to my world, inside my head, where the two boys behind me weren't burning holes on my back.

*You aren't. Not yet.*

Twice Jason has promised retribution, and something tells me he isn't one to make idle threats.

The teacher doesn't have to do much to get the class settled. Half the class is swooning over the guy. He's young, and good-looking I suppose, though not my type.

"I'm Lennox Green," he says in a rich, soothing voice. He has the perfect voice for soliloquies. The sound is so smooth, I want him to keep talking.

Because he's new, he makes us introduce ourselves one by one, calling us out alphabetically. There goes his appeal.

Jason is the first to go—he's an Alden. He leans against his desk, hands in his pockets, and smiles at the teacher.

Fuck.

I've never seen a smile more fake. His eyes remain ice cold, like a snake's.

"I'm Jason, but my mom calls me Jace, after some book she read to me as a child." The girls fawn over him. If my eyes rolled any harder in my skull, they might just fall out. "I play football—tight end. I'll follow in my father's footsteps someday, and join the Senate."

Of course he will, spoiled-ass rich kid. He'll be given the reins of our country like it's his legacy, just like this school.

I tap my pencil on my notebook impatiently, frustrated with myself for paying any attention to his presentation. Who cares? Certainly not me.

I get back to my drawing, only pausing when Mr. Green calls my name. I would have preferred avoiding standing up, but I do as instructed. "I'm Nadia. I like art, I guess."

What else was there to know about me? Nothing much, so I flop down in my chair.

Though I'm not the only one who stuck to the basics, Mr. Green pushes me. "What sort of art, Nadia?"

Resentment rampant, I glare at his pretty face. The teacher's sandy blond, with a beard and rectangular glasses. Is he even old enough to be qualified?

"Anything I can do with my hands." I shrug.

"I can give you something to do with your hands," someone calls suggestively from the back.

I glance over my shoulder. One of the baseball jocks, Martin Lee, holds my gaze as he makes a rude gesture, pumping his fist over his lap. I want to flip him off, but I'm in class, so I do the next best thing. "I'd help if you can find tweezers small enough to hold your junk."

Melina bursts out laughing, along with most of the class. Lee looks furious, and I couldn't give a fuck.

I can't help but notice Cain and Jason. They're glancing at each other, silently communicating in a way that makes me nervous. I feel like they're taking notes, getting to know what makes me tick, preparing to strike where it hurts. I'm getting paranoid.

"All right, all right," Mr. Green says. "Next, Brittany Stevens."

I tune the class out again.

"This year, we will be starting with *Romeo and Juliet*." To emphasize his point, he holds up his own copy of the play.

While I roll my eyes but keep my mouth shut, several guys groan or mutter to each other. Not everyone appreciates Shakespeare. I have my favorites, and *Romeo and Juliet* is not one of them.

Cain's the one to speak up loud enough to be heard over everyone else. "Do you plan on making us study romantic crap for the rest of the year?" His chair squeaks, and I glance at him. He's leaning back in his chair so much that he's in danger of tipping over. Except boys like him never did. The universe simply won't allow it. "I'd like some stuff with murder to balance it out."

Doesn't he know anything about *Romeo and Juliet*? My snort comes just as the class stops chuckling, so to my dismay, Mr. Green notices me. "You have an opinion, Miss Reyes?" he asks, lifting his chin.

This is bullshit. Half the class was agreeing or laughing with Cain. I close my eyes. "It's just that *Romeo and Juliet* isn't exactly romantic. And there's plenty of murder."

"It's viewed by the general population as the most romantic story of all time."

The general population is stupid, then. I'm too frustrated with this entire day to use a filter. "It's a bullshit story about a miscommunication that could have been sorted out with one grown-up conversation but ended up a huge mess because everyone was immature."

There's a snort behind me. When I twist, I meet Jason's cool gaze.

I don't ask anything. I pray he'll drop it. The last thing I need is to interact with him again today. Even in class.

I've been uneasy since the locker incident, waiting for the other shoe to drop. Being so close to him was unnerving enough. Communicating with him...no.

I'd apologize—properly, this time—then we'd go back to a world where we can pretend the other doesn't exist. At least, he could pretend I don't exist. I've never failed to notice him.

"You're immature if you think that." I notice that when he speaks publicly, his voice is very much like his father's. That of a politician, with an undercurrent of power that demands everyone come to heel and listen and obey. Jason's father is a well-known, well-loved senator, who might just have a shot at the presidency.

Picture perfect, with a dash of rot underneath.

I want to drop the subject. Mr. Green doesn't let me. "Nadia speaks rather confidently—I'd wager she can defend her opinion."

Of course I can. That doesn't mean I want to. Because of my teacher's expectant gaze, I blurt out, "Would it have ended the same way had Romeo manned up and simply asked for Juliet's hand?" Staring at Mr. Green rather than Jason emboldens me. "The benefit of a marriage through more traditional means would have ended the war. They merely had to talk to her father directly. Juliet's father wanted her married well, and Romeo's lineage was as good as Paris's."

Mr. Green laughs. “Who’s taking notes? She’ll earn you a straight A, this one.”

My cheeks feel hot.

“Then you rate pretty girls rather generously, sir,” Jason replies.

In another world, I might have just fainted to hear myself called pretty by *him*, but I know it’s meant as an insult right now—he might as well have said I’m an airhead. He didn’t mean it one bit.

“Nadia’s forgetting the type of man Juliet's father was. He beat Juliet for merely suggesting she didn't want to wed his chosen man. Her father wasn't reasonable enough to have accepted a proposal from his enemy’s son."

I pause, because what I remember of the play suggests he might not be entirely wrong. I guess the irritatingly good-looking asshole behind me is more than just a pretty face. How does he know the play so well? I had to study it in a performing arts class I attended last summer, but I couldn’t reconcile my idea of Jason Alden with a Shakespeare lover.

I’m frowning when I find an argument, now unwilling to let this go. It would feel too much like losing. I might rank much lower than Jason in our school ecosystem, and in the real world, too, but here, in AP literature, I’m supposed to be in my domain. Besides, I feel protected by Mr. Green's silent encouragement. Nothing can happen to me in a classroom, right? "Juliet's father wasn't unreasonable as much as he was sexist. Who knows? He might have listened to a man."

Mr. Green claps his hands together once, and then rubs them greedily. I have to admit, he's rather endearing now that I can tell how much of a nerd he is. He's loving this. "Now this is exactly the kind of discussion I want to hear later, once everyone has read the play. *Read* the play," he stresses, turning to the rest of the class. "I do not want you to watch any of the movies."

I'm free—this stupid debate is over. I don't have to glance back or speak to Jason again—directly or otherwise.

My heart is racing. Why does it feel as if I've just run a marathon? All I did was verbally spar with Jason freaking Alden.

After threatening him earlier this morning.

Whose life am I living? It doesn't feel like mine. For two entire years, we haven't interacted, and now, we're enemies, in and out of class.

Mr. Green calls out the name of another student and asks them to read the prologue. He fumbles and stumbles his way through it, and I cringe, barely able to pay attention to the words. I wish our teacher could read it himself.

Something small and hard presses between my shoulder blades. Fully aware of who sits behind me, I ignore it for as long as possible, but the uncomfortable pressure turns into pain, so I shift uncomfortably.

It was a fountain pen.

Who the fuck writes with a fountain pain?

Jason freaking Alden, that's who.

Just as I'm about to ask what he wants, Jason leans forward and passes me a note.

I rush to accept it so our teacher doesn't see us. When Mr. Green has his back to me, I risk opening the note. In a rushed but perfectly elegant scrawl are the words, "These violent delights have violent ends."

I close my eyes, willing this nonsense away.

That makes the third threat I've received in as many hours.

# CHAPTER SEVEN

When the bell rings at the end of class, I'm ready. I've spent the last half hour ruminating on what I should say, and my speech is near perfect in my mind.

I gather my things as fast as I can.

Too slow.

Jason and Cain are both already heading out, joining Lee and the other baseball jocks.

*Fuck.*

I need to catch them and soon, before I lose my mind.

From one moment to the next, I rerun through everything that happened this morning between Judith and the four, either reasoning that things can't be as bad as I thought for me, or deciding I'm screwed.

I can't catch up to them physically. They're all over six feet tall and my reasonable five-five can't match their pace, unless I jog up to them, which would be too humiliating for words. I give up for now.

I meet Sophia at our usual spot, between the cafeteria and the entry hall, and we head inside the cafeteria, chatting about our respective classes.

"I think you'll like Green."

She wrinkles her nose. "I'm not the book nerd here."

Sophia aces lit class, like everything else, but she hates every second of it.

"The teacher has a panty-melting voice, and he's not uneasy on the eyes."

That gets her attention. "Wait, you think he's hot?"

Yeah, no. "I didn't exactly say hot."

"*Not uneasy on the eyes*," she quotes, imitating my voice, a tad lower than hers. "That's basically a love declaration from you."

I'm not that bad; I've just never shown an interest in guys here, because my bank balance makes me unappealing. I have eyes, I can look. Most of our students are pretty, of course—they're rich and that's almost the same thing. If their daddy was ugly, he had a wallet big enough to afford to include pretty in his gene pool, and if all else failed, the kids went under the scalpel before they could walk. But I don't see the point in giving them much of my attention when at best, I'll only be some conquest they can screw and forget the next day. Why waste my energy?

Seniors eat first, so the cafeteria is rather empty;

juniors and sophomores will walk in after half an hour, and freshman in an hour.

Sophia and I grab our trays and make our way to collect our food. There's almost no line, for the first time I can remember.

"Curry," she growls. "You'd think they'd start the year without the torture."

Sophia claims she likes "real curry." She'd been to India three times, and the chef her parents employed was well versed in international cuisine, so she had little patience for our bland facsimile.

I wasn't that fussy.

The cafeteria always offered one main meal as well as a half-dozen alternatives—including sandwiches for anyone in a rush, vegetarian, vegan, halal, kosher, nut-free, and gluten-free options—but most of the staff's effort went toward the principal dish. I didn't hesitate to pick up a bowl of fragrant curry on rice; my standards are far less exacting than Sophia's. I take a water and a yogurt, passing on the starter. Though she pouts, she picks the same combo, and we quietly walk to our usual table.

Our friends scoot over to make room for us, and we sit down.

I say "friends" in the broad sense of the term. We chat at lunch, and we're civil outside of it, but I've kept in touch with none of them except Sophia this summer. We don't have much in common, other than the fact that we're all at the bottom of the hierarchy of Cross for one reason or another. I get the feeling that most of us are academically inclined, and perhaps on the nerdier side, but I don't know them all that well.

"Hey, twinset," Elisa Martin says with an easy smile. She waves, and I can't believe how tanned she is. Her skin is naturally darker, but now it's stunningly black. "We were just talking about the summer. Did you go anywhere nice?"

"Oh, no, tell us where *you* went first!" I demur, hoping to keep the conversation away from me because I didn't go anywhere at all this summer except to work. "I've never seen you this tanned."

"Egypt, to my mother's family, then Namibia. We went to see lions. It was amazing," she gushes.

The destination choice sounds incredible, but that's also why she's at our table: most of the school would have gone to the Caribbean or Europe.

Alexander Burdon leans forward. He's a chess wiz—so good he's won world championships. No one in this school wants to play him—so there's no need to explain why he's with us. "I went to China," he says, "then Japan and Australia. Chess competitions."

"Sophia?" I say, turning to my best friend, still keeping the conversation well away from me. "Tell them all about Europe."

Her eyes brighten. "It was incredible. Would've been more so without my sister, but no one let me push her off the Eiffel Tower."

"What is the point in having a tower that tall if not getting rid of evil siblings?"

I used to think I wanted a sibling, but I'm happy

as an only, all things considered. If there was even the sliver of a chance they might turn out to be anything like Brooke, I'll pass. Besides, Lucas might as well be my brother. We grew up together, spending a good five days out of seven in the same house, taken care of by the same nanny when Mom was busy. It wasn't until here that we drifted apart, because he's hot, popular, and rich, and I'm me. Still, we hang out occasionally.

I haven't seen him at all today. I probably won't. He hardly ever shows up on campus. He almost has enough credits to graduate early, and his attendance requirements are flexible, taking into account his internship at his father's PR firm. Part of me wonders if he would have enrolled at all this year if not for me.

I could have used him today, after my run-in with the four assholes. He doesn't have quite as much clout as they do here, but he's a shield I could brandish to soften whatever blow might be coming...

At least until he disappeared again.

I'm a terrible friend. I completely zoned out as Sophia talked. I've heard all of this before, but that's no excuse.

"You're Willow, right?" Sophia asks a redhead at the other end of the table. Her stunning wavy hair falls a few inches past her shoulders. Her eyes are sky blue, and freckles dot all over her face; I'd bet that the red's natural. "We have Computer Sciences together."

The girl nods. I think she's new, because I can't place her face, but our school is big, with over three hundred students per grade, and I'm not exactly a social animal. Still, she stands out. I'd like to think I would have noticed.

"Did you do anything fun this summer?" Sophia asks.

"I bussed tables," she replies evenly, matter-of fact. "And took care of my brother when I wasn't working."

I immediately feel like an ass. It wasn't that I was ashamed of working; I just hated the looks of pity that usually came with the admission. "I worked too," I rush to confess, so she'll feel normal. "Café or restaurant?"

"An ice cream parlor. The tips were pretty good."

"They usually are in the—"

I don't finish because, without warning, liquid drenches me. Sputtering, I sit there as the coldness slides down my front. Sophia grabs napkins from the trays around us and hands them to me, but I'm frozen, mouth gaping and eyes fixed on the boy who just chucked his smoothie at me.

I say boy and I mean it this time. Though he's tall, ridiculously bulky, and outwardly mature, his playful eyes and mocking smirks are all childish mannerisms. This is a game to him. I can feel a bit slide down my shirt between my breasts. It's fucking cold, so it takes everything in me not to shudder, but I refuse to show any hint of weakness in front of him.

Them.

The other three are standing just paces away, watching me. Cain looks bored. Maverick, exasperated or impatient, I can't quite tell. And Jason...

Jason's cold. Colder than the ice on my skin.

"Oops," Rowan says, all smiles. "I didn't see you there. You're so inconsequential you're practically invisible."

"Grow up, asshole," I shoot back before I can think.

He leans forward. "You know, you could play nice, make this easy for yourself. If you remove your top, do a little dance and sit on my lap, you and I are good. How does that sound, sweet cheeks?"

What the hell?

"You're delusional." I don't understand him. It's not like he wants me—if he did, he would have flirted a little, asked me out. Not...whatever this is. Intimidation, I suppose.

"And you, my dear, are dead meat if you don't get yourself some protection. Enjoy the next year in hell."

I don't understand him then.

The next hour, I do.

## CHAPTER EIGHT

I have enough time to catch a quick shower in my new dorm room. While small, the room's cozy, with dark wood and cream paint. My stuff's already been brought upstairs by maintenance. I slip into another uniform and race back in order to avoid being late for the second time on my first day. Though I suppose I just didn't turn up, the first time.

I feel a little foolish in the locker room right before gym, changing again, especially since I'll also have to grab another shower. But no way was I walking around with sticky banana and kiwi all over me.

I eye the other students gathered outside around the football field, eager to find a familiar face here. There was Sophia in Italian and Melina in English, but no such luck here. I'm in this class with Brooke, along with her friends Yuki Moore and Jacqueline Billington—both legacies. This holy trinity of bitches are the queens of this school. Great.

I also notice the asshole from English, Martin Lee, with a few of his friends. A little late, I see Willow. I didn't notice her with her hair tied up in a ponytail, when it had been loose at lunch. I wave. She waves back, but stays where she is. I consider going to her, in the bleachers, but the teacher's eager to start.

While most of the teachers were all about chatting, today Mr. Pierson is all about launching straight into the torture.

"Take five laps around the field, then we'll grab balls."

I wonder at what age old people forget what it's like to be eighteen. The class chuckles as the baser minds emphasize their desire to have their balls grabbed.

"Congratulations, Lee, you've just earned another lap." The teacher blows his high-pitched whistle before screaming, "Go, go, go!"

No wonder I quit track. There was a second teacher, Mrs. Aspen, but Pierson took the fun right out of life.

As we jog slowly, I start to make my way to Willow, when out of nowhere, someone pushes me from the back. I just have enough balance to catch my footing before I fall, but a foot appears in my way, tripping me over.

"Fuck!" I scream as I fall, bringing my arms before my face to protect it.

Holy fuck, that hurt.

Aching all over, I roll with a wince. My knees are badly scraped, and so are my arms. I hurt my wrist, too, though I don't think it's sprained—I can move it without adding any pain. Thank fuck it's the right one. I'm left-handed—I can still draw.

"Serves you right, bitch," a girl I've never talked to spits at me, her expression half disgust, half fury.

She's downright furious. At me. Although we've never interacted. I don't even know her name.

I'm too stunned to reply.

Two powerful legs in tiny shorts appear in front of me.

"What sort of language is that, Reyes?"

I blink, baffled. I was just pushed, tripped deliberately, and my teacher was upset about my language?

"I fell," I explain, in case he missed it.

"That doesn't excuse what just came out of your mouth. Detention tonight."

My mouth falls open.

What. The. Hell.

"I need to go to the infirmary." I'm no professional—someone needs to check my wrist, and disinfect the rest. "Sir," I add as an afterthought.

He can't deny me that. Right?

"I'll take her," Lee offers with a broad grin.

"Hell no," I shoot back, painstakingly getting to my feet. "I'll take myself, thank you."

"You'll do as you're told, Reyes."

He can't be fucking serious.

"I'm not going alone with that guy." I shake my head, refusing to budge as I get to my wobbly feet. "But I *am* going to the nurse's office to see to the wounds I got in your class. Don't worry—I'll stop by the dean on my way to give a *full* account of what happened here."

I'm not a doormat. I won't be intimidated by any bully—even a fifty-year-old, two hundred pound one.

He grins, showing gray, uneven teeth that make me yearn for mouthwash. "You do that."

I walk away with my head high, eyes forward, refusing to show weakness to the pack of assholes around me.

Fuck them.

Fuck them all.

And fuck the assholes who had them gang up on me. I have zero doubt that this comes from the four assholes. Mr. Pierson was always a dick, but this? It's new, and the timing couldn't be more obvious.

# CHAPTER NINE

My wrist's just bruised, not sprained. That, I expected. The utter indifference of the faculty when I asked to file a report came as a complete surprise, though.

After the nurse, I head straight to the administrative building and ask to see Ms. Casey. Ushered to her office for the second time today, I sit and wait a minute for the young-ish, dark-haired assistant to walk in with a steaming cup of coffee. She smiles at me, but the easiness in her expression of this morning is gone. It's forced. Something tightens in my stomach before I have a chance to say a word.

"Nadia. Back already?"

I nod tightly. "An incident occurred with my PE teacher that I'd like to report. I was tripped over and hurt." I lifted my arms so she could see the bandages on my elbows, and I explain how the asshole resisted my going to get some care after that.

Part of me hesitates, but in the end, I don't bother to mention the ones who kicked me down in the first place, knowing there's nothing the school can do for me on that front—especially after one incident, and when I can't name the perpetrators. I didn't get a look at the person who pushed me from the back, or at the one who moved their foot under me. The best I have is the asshole who called me a bitch, and no one's going to take actions about kids spewing names. Besides, none of them are the real problem.

Part of me wonders whether I should spill everything, though. Today was bullying, and I get the feeling it'll only be the beginning unless I can somehow put a stop to it. But it's their word against mine, and they have more friends than I do. And if, by some sort of miracle, consequences are enforced for the ones who hurt me today, it's likely to rally all their friends against me. I know how this game works. I've seen it often enough with Sophia. Ms. Casey can't help me with my peers. She can, however, make sure the teachers don't mess up my transcript to please four jerks with deep pockets and shallow souls.

Her smile becomes even more awkward, and she takes a sip from her mug before clearing her throat. "Nadia, swearing is something we take very seriously here at Cross and Roses. It's hardly surprising Mr. Pierson was upset at hearing such language in his class." I open my mouth to reply, but she holds her hand up to stop me. "And it sounds like Mr. Pierson did offer you an escort—just not one of your choosing."

Bull. Shit.

At least this time, I don't say it out loud, but my eyes spell it out. Ms. Casey holds my gaze unwaveringly.

"You're a smart kid, Nadia." She sips more coffee. "With a bright future. Don't throw it away on high school drama."

"I came to you because I'm trying to secure my future." My teeth grit, though I do my best to contain my anger. "It's day one of school, I'm hurt, I got detention, and my teacher is picking on me for no valid reason. That's not okay. My uncle is paying five figures a year to guarantee I go to a school without that sort of..." I want to say shit. Instead, I settle on, "Nonsense."

"Do you know much about this school, Ms. Reyes?"

I see I'm no longer Nadia now. I shrug. "I've attended it for two years without issues such as this, so far."

"I meant the history of Cross and Roses. It's quite fascinating. You see, it was founded by Sylvester Cross some eighty years ago. He and his wife, Briar, were quite prolific—nine children, a year or two apart. They both worked, and quite successfully so, in their respective industries. As you can imagine, things got a little chaotic at home, no matter how many governesses they employed."

I really wish I knew why she thought I'd fucking care, but I knew better than to interrupt her.

"So they decided to ship their children off. There were plenty of boarding schools at the time, but the Crosses were quite particular. Only the best of the best for their precious babies. They chatted with a handful of their friends and business partners, all of whom felt the same way. The following year, this place was built." Her eyes went skyward. "The administrative building was the original school. It expanded over the years, but in the beginning, there were only about fifty children, from thirteen families. The Crosses, of course, and the Montgomerys, the Fullers, the Cushmans..."

My jaw tightens when I understand her point as she names a few of the legacies.

She knows.

Somehow, she knows the mess I'm in right now is coming from *them*. Which means that the assholes' reach goes further than I anticipated.

I won't find any help here.

I twist on my chair. So now what? Should I change schools? Fuck. How did everything go so wrong, so fucking fast?

I open my mouth and close it again, thinking through what I need to say as Ms. Casey looks at me, eyes filled with sorrow. I don't get the impression she wants to be cruel. But she won't help me either. "So what would you suggest I do?"

She perks up, smiling at me again, more genuinely this time. "Well, as you're here, you could pop into Mr. Clark's office and speak about what you can do in that free period to pad your transcript, yes?"

She can't be serious. I have bigger problems right now.

Ms. Casey narrows her eyes on me intently. "See, if there's one thing no one can take from you, it's achievements. You historically have a good attendance record, decent grades outside of science, and enough extracurricular activities to make you worth a second look. Keep it up."

I read between the lines.

She's telling me this year is screwed for me, but with my eyes on the prize, I can get out of here with what I need. Admittance to a college of my choosing.

In the meantime, I'm supposed to suck it up.

*Fuck.*

# CHAPTER TEN

The last week fucking sucked.

There was a mix-up because Sophia *was* told we'd be roommates yesterday morning, but when she turned up after school, she'd been paired with a sophomore It girl wannabe. She was pissed, and after the day I'd had I couldn't deal with the series of rants she sent, so I ignored her to take a nap. I woke up to over a hundred messages I didn't even bother trying to read. In the morning, she gave me the cold shoulder on the bus.

Just *great*.

Tuesday, I walked in to find my locker spray painted with dicks and the word "whore"—because high school bullies are *oh so mature*—and then I had to endure Cain and Jason's presence at my back later, knowing they were behind it.

My hands were clenched into fists during the entire hour. I had my stuff packed before the bell rang and darted out of there. I didn't bother to wait for Sophia—I'd have to deal with her annoyance later. Besides, I was rather upset with her myself. I checked her texts; she hadn't so much as asked why I hadn't answered, or if anything was going on with me. But I realized deep down that I was probably misplacing my anger.

I grabbed a sandwich and marched right out of the cafeteria, heading to the gardens at the back of the school. Though we were in early September, the weather was crappy enough for the wolves to have stayed indoors. Indifferent to the rain, I sat on a bench shielded by a pruned cedar.

The highlight of my day was spotting the black stray cat that sometimes hangs out around there.

The infirmary gave me the week off PE to ensure my wrist heals, but I showed up to class anyway, to show Pierson and the rest of the assholes I'm not afraid.

The rest of the week was spent anticipating the worst, dodging "accidental" hits, and ignoring insults. It took two more days for Sophia to realize something is seriously wrong and corner me as I rushed out of the cafeteria again. I didn't get into details, too tired to bother.

"The four assholes at the popular table declared me persona non grata. It's hell."

"That sucks. You should come to the table, eat with us. They can't do much in front of everyone, right?"

I lifted my brow, vividly remembering the

smoothie incident. It wasn't the worst thing that happened this week—not by a long shot—but they'd had no problem doing it in front of the entire cafeteria, supervisors included.

"I'll pass." Just as I turned to leave, I caught his eyes.

Jason.

He looked at me every day—not constantly, but half of the times when I found myself checking on the four predators feasting on my misery, he was staring.

In another lifetime, I would feel flattered, but I know he's just amusing himself, trying to see if I'm close to breaking.

Which I'm not.

This petty bullshit sucks, but Ms. Casey was right. I'll survive the school drama. I just need to keep my eye on the light at the end of the tunnel.

None of the four guys have approached me at all since Rowan's lewd suggestion on Monday. They don't need to. They've declared open season on me—that's enough. Most of the senior class rushed to do their bidding.

I had a better opinion of humanity before this week. Even seeing Sophia's experience, I'd still thought that people were mostly good, assuming that there were only a few jerks in every group. Sophia's harassed by her sister and a couple of her friends—three of them against two of us. It kinda felt...fair, I suppose. But almost the entire school hates me simply because four overly privileged asses told them to. Now, I'm not so sure I believe in us as a species. We're sheep. I keep my head high, not even checking who's calling me, knocking against my shoulder, or telling my teachers I'm doing something I'm not supposed to—mostly, drawing. None of the teachers really care, thankfully. The only asshole is Pierson.

Though far from indifferent to the ordeal, I make a good show of hiding any weakness. At least, I think I do.

Friday is better and worse all at once. My stuff was taken from my locker during PE, which sucked. I don't mind so much about the uniform—I just wear my PE clothes in my art class. No one cares in art. That hour has become a solace in the last week. None of the sheep make it through the doors.

I do, however, care about losing my backpack. It was a birthday present from Mom. Plus, I'll have to use my hard-earned greenbacks to replace my bag and its contents.

At least I had the sense to keep my phone in my pocket, and my cards and IDs are in its case.

For all that, Friday's much better because Lucas is back. My cousin has been absent until now, and as usual, his texts are never forthcoming.

I run into his arms and squeeze a little too hard, considering I saw him a week ago. Then I playfully punch his shoulder. "Good of you to show up."

He makes a show of shielding his face with his forearms, inviting me to take another shot. And I do.

We had boxing lessons together in junior high. Lucas's been two heads taller than me, and perhaps twice as broad, for the last decade, but I still win against him, because he has some stupidass rule about not hitting girls.

After the third lackluster punch, he grabs my wrist and twists it behind my back, moving to get me in a headlock. I laugh as I break out of it.

It's our usual greeting. I know what he's doing. Though it's playful and neither of us are using much strength, he's being a paranoid, protective guy like his dad, and making sure I haven't forgotten how to fight, how to get away from an intruder.

I'm just Uncle Lucius's niece, but he's made millions, and he comes from a family with a certain reputation. His own work isn't the safest. Having Astrella blood means I could be in danger someday, and I've been prepared for it.

Too bad my uncle didn't prepare me to fight school bullies as well as potential kidnappers.

"They don't give a fuck if I'm here or not, as long as Dad keeps the money coming," Lucas reminded me. Then he smirks. "And I keep raising their average."

Annoyingly true. Lucas is my opposite, useless at anything remotely creative, but he's smart. Crazy smart. He's never needed to work to ace his tests. Rich, brainy, and though it pains me to admit it, attractive, he has it all. I'd hate him if I didn't love him so much.

He falls into step beside me, and I head toward

my locker. He walks with a swagger, casual yet utterly arrogant all at once. More than a few girls—and a couple guys—check him out, freshman whispering and giggling, older students trying to catch his eyes. His hair bounces slightly, the strands dark and wavy, a bit longer on the top. He looks too much like my father and his for me to be affected, but I know what they see.

He tilts his chin toward my locker as we approach. The dicks have been scrubbed, but they're still visible—as is the lovely inscription. "I see someone's starting the year right." There's some humor in his eyes, until he sees me enter my combination and realizes it's my locker.

His jaw tightens, his eyes narrowing.

"Don't get involved," I tell him, before he can manage a word. "You'll make everything worse. They'll forget about me and move on to another target soon."

Right? They have to.

His hazel eyes, similar to mine, though they're more interesting, burn a bright green when he says between clenched teeth. "You're not a *target*. You're an *Astrella*." He says this like the name should matter, and to him, it does. I don't navigate Uncle Lucius's world enough to be impressed by it, I suppose. "Letting crap happen to you reflects on all of us."

"Well, good thing that my surname is Reyes then," I shoot back coolly. "I mean it. Leave it be. You're only here two days a week at best. If you interfere, you're going to make things worse for me when you're not looking."

He knows I'm right, though he doesn't like it. Lucas glares at me as though I'm somewhat responsible for all this. Which I am, I suppose. But finally, he nods.

I hold his gaze, not really trusting him to let this go.

"Why didn't you text me?" There's an accusatory tone I don't appreciate.

Now I roll my eyes. "You never answer texts."

"I do when they're important—there's a difference between asking me what I think about a stupidass show and letting me know someone's causing trouble for you." He pauses. "Is there more?"

I'm glad my tights and blazer cover my knees and elbows—the scrapes are scabbed but still visible.

Rather than answering, I tell him, "I have been and can continue to handle myself, but I'd rather avoid escalations. Stay out of it." I slam my locker shut and give Lucas a huge smile as if to prove everything's fine. "I'm good. Promise."

I kiss his cheek and wave before departing for my next class.

It'll probably be a week before I see him again, which is for the best, because I *do* want him to ignore all of this. Seeing him was enough to cheer me up.

Before he disappears at the end of the corridor, Lucas turns to me. "Hey! I forgot. Catch!" He chucks something in the air, and I have to jump in an attempt to intercept it. It falls to my right. Bending down to grab it, I smile.

My car keys.

Hulk is here.

## CHAPTER ELEVEN

I tend to stay on campus most weekends. Underclassmen need to have permission slips to leave during the term—even on weekends—but no one asks for them. The school encourages students to remain, so they can participate in group projects and socialize with their peers. No one protests, because the weekends at Cross are fun. There are games, races, competitions, and parties—some sanctioned by the school, others not so much. Even outliers like Sophia and I enjoy weekends.

This week, I practically run out the doors the moment the last bell rings on Friday. Not even bothering to change out of my uniform, I race past the dorm, heading for the parking lot at the gatehouse.

I close in on Hulk just as a limo glides into the parking lot.

My heart skips a beat, then drums too fast in my chest. I know that car. It's not the longest, or the flashiest of the legacies' vehicles. The dark red Bentley is classic, standing out among the rest.

Jason's car.

Cain's the first to come out, followed by Maverick and Rowan. They're joking around, as if all is right in the world. I suppose it is, for them.

I should get inside Hulk and get the hell out of here. I should...

They've seen me now. Maverick elbows Rowan and tilts his head at me. Cain's smirking, eyes fastened on me.

No sign of Jason so far. If he's in the car, I can't tell—the windows are tinted nearly black.

"Well, if it isn't our pretty little girl." Cain has the nerve to wink at me.

What a fucking dick. "Do you get off on terrorizing little girls, asshole?"

*Shut it. Get. In. The. Car.*

But my legs don't obey me. Nor does my mouth.

I lift my chin. "I told you I was sorry I got in your face on Monday. That didn't matter to you, did it? You love causing pain too much to waste any opportunity." All of my anger and frustration of the week's coming out in waves, whether I want it to or not. "Let me guess, Mummy and Daddy didn't pay enough attention to you, so you bully people for no reason? You're pathetic."

I'm making things worse for myself. I'm also past caring. Each ugly word crossing my lips makes me feel a little less helpless, grasping at strands of power. I can almost feel a smile curving my lips as I detect unease from the three assholes. They exchange a certain look that carries meaning.

"Good guess. Two out of four." I'd recognize that voice anywhere. Jason.

I blanch, completely unprepared. He's right behind me, although I never saw him come out of the car.

I don't want to turn, unwilling to let them circle me, but I can't help glancing over my shoulder.

My jaw would have hit the ground if I'd let my expression show. The man behind me looks nothing like the Jason I'm used to. He's far, far worse.

Clad in denim and leather, he leans over a sexy, sultry bike—a black BMW with red accents—holding a helmet in his left hand.

He and his friends don't look like boys, unlike most of the seniors; their athletic regimen gave them broad shoulders, strong legs, and muscles no eighteen-year-old had the right to possess. Right now, Jason's all man, all dangerous, and fucking delicious.

I would never have imagined this, not in my wildest dreams. To me, Jason always wears a shirt, probably a tie, if not a custom-made tuxedo. He's supposed to be preppy, appropriate—a mini-senator.

He tilts his head. "My parents are pretty cool. So are Maverick's. Cain's are too wrapped up in themselves to pay attention to their kid, though, so you get full credit for that. As for Rowan's—they're dead, so yeah, I suppose they're not paying attention to him. His grandparents are sweet, though."

I feel awful, just as Jason intended, but I don't let it show. "Everyone has their issues. Not everyone chooses to torment others in order to make themselves feel better."

Jason grins. It's almost friendly, devoid of the coldness I'm used to. "Is that what you think we're doing, cupcake?"

"Stop calling me that."

He leaves the helmet on the seat of his bike and prowls toward me. My hand tightens on the door handle of my car as I see the other three close in too.

The parking lot has started to fill, though. We're not alone. They can't hurt me in front of a crowd and get away with it.

*Can't they?*

I ignore the uneasiness in my stomach, and the voice at the back of my mind reminding me that they did exactly that all week.

And they're still approaching me.

I open the car and slide into my seat, closing the door just as Jason reaches me. I lock it, exhaling in relief. It takes another breath to realize that the move made me look like a coward.

Jason casually knocks on the window.

I could start the car and get out of here.

But what about Monday, and the day after that, and the day after that?

I roll the window down halfway. "What?"

"You didn't answer the question."

I hadn't? I couldn't even remember the question. "Refresh my memory."

"Is that what you believe we're doing? Tormenting you."

He must be kidding.

"You made this week hell for me, and you know it."

That wasn't quite right, though. The only time I'd dealt directly with Their Majesties was Monday. Since then, they've let their minions terrorize me on their behalf.

They aren't the kind of people who get their hands dirty.

"Cupcake." His fingers tap gently against the window. "We've done nothing to you. Yet."

"Why don't you find another toy to play with?"

Jason leans in. "Because this one is still shiny, and not broken. I'd very much like to see what you look like when all your pieces fall apart."

Enough of this. I close the window, start the car, and reverse out of the lot, paying them no more attention. I have two days to myself before returning to the hell they've designed for me. Freedom can't start soon enough.

# CHAPTER TWELVE

I don't rest. Not for a moment the entire weekend.

My mother drills me about why I chose to come back, missing any homecoming parties. I know better than to let her know about the mess at school; parents can never fix that sort of thing. They could kick up a fuss with the school, sure, which might result in Their Majesties getting a slap on the wrist, at worst—and then they'd know I snitched and push me harder.

My interaction with Jason and the others Friday night keeps me awake. I don't like the person I was that evening. I've never shown those ugly colors, not even to Brooke. I'm not cruel by nature, yet I tried to be. They dragged me down to their level.

Rowan's eyes feature in my waking nightmares, because for a fraction of a second, I'm fairly certain I saw some hurt. His parents are dead and I'd made fun of them. Indirectly, unknowingly, but it was still an asshole move. All he did was chuck a smoothie at me. I'd wager my words cut deeper than his actions.

Then I remember being tripped, pushed, insulted, spat on, and I shake the guilt away.

*We've done nothing to you. Yet.*

I take a shift at the restaurant Saturday. Septembers are always busy in the city, so Dad doesn't hesitate when I ask if he could use an extra set of hands. I'm grateful for the distraction, not to mention the money I earn that night. It's not much, but it'll pay for my backpack and the stuff I lost.

*Yet. Yet. Yet.*

Jason's promise turns around my mind on repeat as dread coils inside me, tightening as the hours draw me closer to Monday.

Naturally, Hulk works just fine that morning. Part of me wishes I could break down and wait on the side of the road for a tow for...a few months? Just until graduation. But I make it on time.

I bought a new pair of headphones along with my replacement backpack. They're noise cancelling. The expense might have seemed superfluous, but this morning, they're my lifeline. I listen to a book, blocking out any whispers or snickering that might be aimed at me.

I head to my locker first—someone had cleaned it properly over the weekend. Opening it, I sigh. I should have guessed. I can't tell whether it's been filled with whipped cream or shaving cream. Either way, it's unusable. I don't have time to head to the administrative building if I want to make it to class on time, so I just snap a picture, load it to SnapApp, and tag the school before heading down the corridor toward my calculus class. Some random kid bumps into me—maybe purposely, maybe not. Since I'm not in the mood to take more crap, I shoot him the finger. One week of it was more than enough. Now, if they want to fuck with me, I'll fuck them right back.

That sounds dirtier than intended.

The next couple of hours are tolerable. Calculus sucks by nature, but my fellow students leave me alone; I suppose they deem the class torture enough for anyone. I sit next to Sophia in Italian. We didn't talk much over the weekend. Before class starts, she asks me how my shift went.

"Really well. I got good tips." The universe must have decided that I'd suffered enough to deserve some boon, because I served a bunch of drunk dudes who tipped me thirty percent on their twenty-five head table. "Did you have a good time here?"

Sophia's parents take a vacation every year around this time—to celebrate their kids going back to boarding school, I'm guessing—so she had to stay. Any other week, I would have asked if she wanted to come back to mine, but I really needed the break. My work shift was a good excuse for not inviting her.

"Amazing." To my surprise, she's beaming. "Yuki invited me to Glass Sunday afternoon. You wouldn't *believe* how gorgeous the house is. And they have butlers! And a spa! We did mani-pedis." She wiggles her fingers at me.

My eyebrows are up to my hairline by that point. There's only one Yuki I know who's a legacy, but I have to clarify. "Yuki Moore?"

Sophia's sister might be the aspiring queen bee of Cross, but Yuki Moore, the gorgeous, smooth-skinned, raven-haired, ink-eyed model-worthy beauty rules it without even trying. Yuki lets Brooke have her fun—she doesn't seem to have an interest in leading the mean girl squad—but what she says goes. Brooke immediately bows to every one of Yuki's words.

And *she* invited Sophia? It just didn't make any sense to me.

"She's pretty nice, actually. She wants to be a lawyer, like her mom, so she's taking so many AP classes, she doesn't really bother with the school drama, you know."

I didn't know anything about Yuki, other than the fact that she was super-mega rich and extremely gorgeous.

And, all right, I *might* have noticed the fact that she dated Jason for a bit. But only because Jason doesn't date. Oh, I've seen him make out with one girl or another at some weekend parties, but he doesn't seem to give them the time of day afterwards. Yuki, he speaks to, sometimes hangs out with.

She's never spoken a word to me, or to Sophia

before, and all of a sudden, they're spa buddies? That can't be good.

Italian flies by too fast, because in no time, I have to go to my English class.

I arrive before Jason and Cain, and debate sitting in a different seat. There aren't assigned seats in the class, although everyone has stayed in the same seats since the first day of class. The ones up front are all claimed, but there's a seat to the left that doesn't have seats available behind it, so I take it. It's Monday. I'm allowed a little cowardice on Monday.

I should've realized that wouldn't stop the assholes. I sink in my seat when Jason and Cain walk in, but they make a beeline for me. Cain continues to the next row, but Jason hovers beside me.

I try not to tense too obviously.

"You know Lucas," he comments casually, as though it was the most natural thing in the world.

*Shit.* I seriously hope my cousin kept his word. I need him to stay out of this mess before it escalates. I don't answer.

Jason sits on a corner of my desk and leans in to me, reaching out to touch my chin.

He lifts it so I meet his eyes. I slap his hand away. "Don't touch me."

He shoots me the ghost of the smile I saw Friday. "Don't ignore me, cupcake. You wouldn't like the consequences."

God, I hate him.

"What's it to you, *Jace*?"

He said his mother calls him that last week. I wanted to piss him off, yet he appears pleased.

"Good question, Nadia." The way he scrutinizes me makes me uncomfortable. Everything about him makes me uncomfortable. "He was at my club this weekend. Mentioned you in passing. He seemed quite possessive."

I'm going to murder Lucas.

Letting Jason think I'm his girlfriend or whatever could work to my advantage—maybe he'd think twice before messing with me—but I can't bring myself to. It's just so gross.

"He's my cousin. We grew up together. Will you go away now?"

Jason frowns, puzzled. "Not from his father's side. I would have met you before, otherwise."

He had.

Just the once.

"Do you want me to draw a family tree?" I smirk, rolling my eyes.

He nods. "If you would be so kind."

I can't make heads or tails of what's going on in that guy's head.

The teacher walks in just as the bell rings. I grab a notebook out of my backpack, along with my new copy of *Romeo and Juliet*.

Jason tilts his head to my bag. "Isn't that a little heavy?"

It's filled to the brim with all my art supplies, gym clothes, and schoolbooks.

"Well, if your sycophants hadn't ruined my locker, I wouldn't have to cart all my books around."

"You know, I could make your life a little easier, provided you play along." He tilts his head.

"What, I tell you about my family and you call off the dogs?"

He shrugs. "I could, for a day or two."

He's basically admitting to controlling the assholes who come after me, but I already knew he was.

Some information for a day or two of peace is a small price to pay. "My dad's his dad's little brother."

"Astrella?" He shakes his head. "I've known Lucas since we were children. You say you grew up together—"

"Mr. Alden, if you would be so kind as to take your seat," Mr. Green demands.

I beam at Jason, glad he's not getting his way for once.

To my surprise, he's entirely ignoring the teacher. "Astrella kept you away from the New York society. Why?"

My jaw tightens. I know the answer, of course. I just don't want to give it to him. "We have class."

Jason keeps his unwavering gaze on mine for what might be seconds or minutes before finally moving.

A chair squeaks, and from the corner of my eye,

I watch a guy shift over. Of course. He made whoever's behind me move.

Fucker.

Mr. Green starts class.

A pencil stabs between my shoulder blades again, just like on the first day of school. I ignore Jason. Without warning, he grabs my hair, and I do my best to continue to ignore him.

Jason yanks my hair harder this time, so hard, and suddenly I scream in surprise.

"Ms. Reyes!" Mr. Green's pissed; his tone is cold for once. "There is no excuse for such behavior."

I think I hate this teacher.

I know I hate this school.

And I sure as fuck hate the guy sitting behind me.

"I'm sorry, Mr. Green," I say between clenched teeth. I want to add that it won't happen again, but with Jason, who knows?

*Transcript. Transcript. Transcript. I'll make it out of here. I will.*

I can hardly concentrate the rest of class, and as soon as it ends, I turn to Jason, fuming. "What the hell do you want?"

"To teach you a lesson," he says, smiling that smile that doesn't reach his intense gray eyes. "Actions have consequences, always. Don't ignore me again."

I don't think, I just act. My hand reaches out to his hair, threads through the golden strands, and I close my fist around a handful of his silky curls.

"How do *you* like it, Jace?" I sneer.

I'm not pulling as hard as he did, but I could. I'm trying to be better than him—if only a little.

I expect him to tell me to stop, to demand it. Jason Alden doesn't *ask*. He might try to break my grip, too. I'm prepared for it, bracing myself for any form of attack.

Or so I thought, before his mouth closes on mine. I gasp under his kiss, letting go of his hair. He takes advantage of my opening, deepening his twisted kiss. His hand moves to my neck, keeping me in place.

I can't move. I can't think. All I can do is feel, feel his touch and his mouth down to the tips of my toes and into my core.

*Fuck.*

I finally push against his chest—too late for my ego's sake. His hold on my neck tightens, and he laughs against my lips.

Then his mouth moves to the corner of my chin, and my jaw, then my neck, and up to my ear. Each kiss is teasing, leisurely, as though I weren't thrashing against him to try to get him off me.

Against my ear, he whispers. "Don't start things with me, cupcake. I'll finish them."

He finally lets go. I turn back to my desk and stuff my books into my bag.

"So, why did Astrella hide you?" Jason asks.

"Fuck you!" My hands are shaking. Sure, I've had more original answers, but my brain isn't working at its best capacity.

Jason Alden kissed me.

"I mean, you could, but I'd still want to know why he hid you afterwards."

I walk out of the classroom as fast as my feet and my pride can carry me.

# CHAPTER THIRTEEN

I don't understand anything for the rest of the day. I have no clue whether we played dodgeball or football. My art class might as well have been calculus for all I retained from it. And as I lie in bed at dinnertime, rehashing my English lesson, I don't understand *him*.

I mean, I suppose I get the curiosity. As a child, I remember my mother getting ready for so many parties where I had to stay behind, although Lucas was allowed to go. We were the same age, so it didn't make sense. As I grew older, I got over it. They were my uncle's parties. He might have to put up with his son, but that didn't mean that he wanted another kid cramping his style. He was always kind to me, but I still was just his niece, not his daughter.

But if Jason and other children of our age had attended, then indeed, it felt like I'd been purposely excluded. I had a theory for that possibility, too:

Lucius was protecting me. Lucas had bodyguards until he was sixteen, and there had been many kidnapping attempts. It wasn't uncommon for the children of wealthy, powerful families. I bet Jason also had bodyguards outside of Cross. It wasn't necessary here because the security of this place was insane—there were hundreds of guards patrolling day and night.

My uncle had been careful to avoid being seen in public with me for a long time so that I could have a normal life. I didn't have bodyguards, or drivers taking me everywhere. If I'd attended Astrella galas, I would have had to. It would have changed my entire way of life. Sure, I attend this fancy school, but outside in the real world, I wait tables, go to concerts with my friends, rollerblade on our local ramp, and paint the occasional graffiti. Lucas, not so much. He has more freedom now that he's proven he's capable of taking care of himself, but our childhood was different.

When we went bowling or mini-golfing, Uncle Lucius booked the entire venue and had guards posted at each entrance. Most days, he stayed home, outside of school hours. Lucas naturally rebelled, which led to Lucius shipping him off to Cross and Roses.

The question is, why does Jason care so much?

Frustrated with myself for letting him get into my head, I decide to take a long hot shower. I'm a little more relaxed by the time I get out—and when my stomach reminds me of its existence, I regret missing out on dinner.

I eat a highly unsatisfying breakfast bar from the stash I keep in my desk drawer for the days when I wake up late, and hop on my bed again, headphones on.

I'm dozing off to the sound of my audiobook, finally letting go of the stress of the day.

Then I open my mouth to scream. There's someone in my room—a tall frame in the darkness. Before I manage to get a sound out, a hand covers my mouth. I kick out and grab the wrist in front of me, ready to break it, when the intruder removes my headphones with his free hand.

"It's me! Jesus, you're feisty."

I calm down some—not much—and flip on the light on my bedside table.

Jason.

What the *fuck* is he doing here in my room, in the middle of the night?

Well, it's probably not that late, considering I crashed as soon as I got back, but he still shouldn't be anywhere near my room. We're not friends. Even if we were friends, it wouldn't be appropriate. Guys aren't allowed in girls' rooms. I'm not blind—or deaf—I know plenty of students trample on that rule, but still.

Heart rate still too rapid, I sit up, bringing my comforter up to my chin. I'm wearing a tank top and tiny PJ shorts that got too small last year.

"What the fuck are you doing here?"

He shrugged. "Wouldn't want you to starve."

I finally notice he's holding a paper bag. As he lifts it to my nose, I'm hit with a delicious scent that makes my mouth water. I'd kill for whatever's in that bag.

"I'm not hungry."

He laughs as my treacherous stomach betrays me, growling like an angry dog.

Dammit. Terrible timing.

"Come on, cupcake. It's just a burger. It won't bite you."

He might.

I don't make a move to take the bag. Jason sighs, dropping it on top of the four books already on my bedside table.

He sits at the foot of my bed and looks around my room as though he has every right to. "Did you draw this?" He gestures to the sketch on the easel that takes up most of my room.

"You should get out. I don't want to get in trouble."

His eyes cut to mine, and he smirks. "Oh, Nadia. If that were true, you wouldn't fight me."

I swallow. He's right. My life was fine before him. Foolish to challenge the king in his court.

"I'm not fighting you," I deny, bringing my knees to my chest.

"Aren't you?" Jason lies back, nonchalant as ever. "Your family. Tell me why they hide you."

I take a deep breath. Giving my enemy information he could use to hurt me goes against my instincts, but I want to play nice. Jason can make sure the others leave me alone if he wants to. I have to try. "My dad isn't rich like Uncle Lucius. He does okay—he owns a restaurant—but some seasons are better than others, you know." I shrug. "I get that my uncle didn't want me to get into your world and put a target on my back."

"Yet here you are," Jason said. "Why send you to Cross?"

"I've been here for two years, and you're the first to even guess I know Lucas."

Jason nods, accepting my point. "Are you jealous of your cousin?" he wonders.

I wrinkle my nose. "Why would I be? You wouldn't believe how hard Lucas works—how hard he's always worked. After school, he had tutors in business and politics, piano, violin, dance..." I wince on his behalf. "I had my freedom."

"Had," Jason agrees. "Now you belong to me."

I stand up, pointing to the door. "Get out of my room now, or I'm going to scream."

He's just staring at me. When his eyes roam down my body, I remember my minimal clothing. I might blush, but I refuse to back down.

"I'll tell them you forced your way in, which you did. Even you can't get away with *that*."

Now, Jason stands up. "Tut-tut. You know I don't like being threatened, cupcake."

# CHAPTER FOURTEEN

I hate him.

I've used the word occasionally, like anyone else, but I've never truly hated anyone until this moment. There's no other word to describe the mixture of intense frustration and fury, tinged with fear.

I cross my arms over my middle, itching to grab my covers and wrap them around myself, but I know I'll look weak if I give into my instinct. Instead, I clench my teeth and repeat, "Get out, Jason."

He grins and, to my surprise, stands up. I expected more of a fight.

I can't help taking a step back. I'm too close to the bed—too close to him. My retreat makes him smile.

For two years, I've never seen him smile. Not once. In the past two weeks, it's happened at least three times. Always in private—when it's just his friends and me. This smile reaches his eyes, and I hate, hate, hate how fucking good he looks. If he smiled like that every day, he would have been number one in the survey last year, no question.

In another world, I might have liked having Jason Alden in my room. But his smile's twisted and he's more dangerous than a snake in the grass.

What he enjoys is my discomfort.

Instead of walking to the door, he strolls toward me. I take another step back and hit the back of my desk's chair. Fuck.

Jason keeps advancing leisurely, as though he has all the time in the world. I wonder if he wants me to run. The sicko might enjoy the chase. I stay put on unsteady legs, counting on bravado and the adrenaline running through my veins to see me through whatever comes next.

Less than a foot away from me, Jason rests his hands on either side of my chair's back, caging me, and leans in. "You know what's wrong with you, Nadia?"

"Right now? The fact that you're in my room. I wasn't joking. I'll scream."

He smirks and shakes his head. "You were born in the wrong bloodline. You're the spawn of the runt of a mildly successful crook, and yet you act like a queen." Somehow, he made it sound like an insult. "You have a backbone of steel. The problem is, steel's too stiff. It doesn't bend well. It breaks."

I bring my knee up to his groin without warning,

but Jason lifts his leg to block it, then presses up against me.

*Oh my god.*

He's hard. There's no mistaking the solid bulge against my stomach. Even through his tailored black school pants and my PJs, I can feel its heat.

I shove against his chest. "Move!"

I don't even gain an inch. I might as well push a stone wall.

"Or you'll scream?" He laughs, digging in his pocket for his phone. "Take a look how that's going to work out for you."

I'm confused when he unlocks it and hands it to me, but I take it, seeing the SnapApp interface.

My mouth falls open.

**I'm wet and ready for you, Jason. Please come fill me with your cum.**

The nasty message is accompanied by a salacious shot of a slender, athletic girl—no face, but I certainly see plenty of everything else. She's lying on a school bed, legs spread, her hands down her minuscule lace panties.

None of that astonishes me—I'm guessing he receives invitations of this sort on a daily basis. What's wrong is that the sender is *me*.

It was received half an hour ago.

If I scream as I've threatened to, all he has to do is show this and whatever I say will be immediately dismissed. I'll be expelled on the spot.

I shake my head. "It's not my profile."

"Isn't it?"

I break his hold—and he lets me, because there's no fighting against his muscles—to rush to my bedside table. I check my phone, heading to SnapApp. Indeed, that filthy message was sent from my account. "What the fuck?"

I'm screwed. How am I supposed to prove this wasn't me?

"You should be more careful. Technology's your enemy." He sounds as blasé as if we were discussing the weather.

"You know, I could make you post this picture publicly. SnapApp might have been designed to keep the users' privacy intact, but you can be certain there'll be screenshots. Maybe someone will send it to your parents. To the colleges you apply to. To your future job... So scream, Nadia. I fucking dare you."

Jason Alden is a monster. I never realized that before. I'm not playing on even ground, because there are no limits as far as he's concerned. He could ruin my life, and he doesn't care.

He leans back on my desk. "Now let's talk about that habit of yours. I told you how I felt about being threatened the first day of school. You've felt the consequences since. And yet, here we are again."

"You're invading my space," I remind him. "I told you what would happen if you didn't go away; that's not a threat, that's you choosing a course of action and me stating its consequences."

"There's that crown again." He flashes me all his teeth. "It seems you missed the memo, so here's how the world works, cupcake. Those in power get away with literal murder. Those without suffer consequences. Your life will be much easier if you accept that simple truth."

Everything in me rebels against his words. I want to scream "No. No. *No*." And yet, part of me knows he's right.

"Speaking of consequences. Back to the threatening thing." He takes his time, eyes tracing from my bare feet to my eyes as I stand dumbly next to my bed. "Lie back and spread your legs, Nadia."

# CHAPTER FIFTEEN

He's fucking kidding. Right? He isn't that much of an asshole.

His eyes gleam with something dark and wild, and I suddenly realize he *is* that much of an asshole. That and more. This is the real Jason, not the cookie-cutter version he presents to the world to become a senator like his father. A selfish, cruel, sadistic dick who loves seeing others suffer.

"Jason..."

"Yes, Nadia?"

I don't know what to say, what to do to get out of this mess. "I'm sorry I got involved that first day. More than you know. I had no idea what was going on; all I saw was a girl in trouble. You understand that, don't you?"

"Perfectly. Lie back."

I bite my lower lip. "Please. We don't have to be enemies. Before this year, you didn't even know I existed. We can go back to that. I'll fade into the background and leave you alone. I promise I won't cause any trouble." I'm bargaining because I know where threats are likely to get me. But every word feels more desperate and hopeless. They're received with cool indifference.

"I know you won't. Lie back."

"*No*."

Silence meets the word at first. Then Jason pushes up from the desk and laughs. "I knew you'd make this entertaining." Shaking his head, he pulls out his phone. "Here's the difference between you and I, cupcake. You make threats. I give warnings. Now, let's get this appealing picture posted..."

I feel sick to my stomach.

The picture isn't of me, but it won't matter. From that angle, it could be any white girl on there, and if I appear to be the one posting it...

"Wait."

I can't let him ruin my future on a whim. I can't let him make me that girl. The one everyone hears about in any town: she was *so* promising, until compromising videos or pictures came up. Fast forward ten years and she's doing porn because no one else would hire her.

She's not me. She won't be. I'll do just about anything to avoid that fate.

And the monster across the room knows it.

He's sick—there's no other explanation. He can have any girl in the school. He could have had me if he'd asked me out instead of what he's been doing since the start of the year. He's blackmailing me because he *likes* it.

"I'm waiting, cupcake."

But I don't move. I don't think I can. I wet my lips, my mind racing as I desperately try to think of a way to escape this.

Finally, I sit on my bed, each beat of my heart resounding in my ears, almost deafening. My legs remain closed.

He wants to make me spread them for him to show just how powerless I truly am. Ripping my thighs apart himself wouldn't send the same message. Jason isn't brutal. He's vicious.

"Why?" I ask.

He tilts his head.

"Why are you making me do this?" I try to understand. Understanding might make this less terrifying and daunting. I'm also playing for time. I don't know what he has planned for me once I comply, but it can't be good for me. "Is that what gets you off? Blackmail?"

He shrugs, unaffected by what I intended as an insult. "Not typically, but right now? Certainly."

I feel a little sick. He finds this arousing.

"Is it about taking control?" I push.

Jason moves. I flinch as he approaches. Him getting closer to me wasn't my intent.

I climb onto my bed, drawing my knees to my chest and move away until my back hits the wall.

"I'm not taking control of you, Nadia. You can make your own choices. Each has its consequences."

He grins, delighted to throw my words back at me. "So what will it be?"

His hands brace on either side of my feet and he bends forward, his face almost reaching mine. "Time's up."

I swallow, my throat feeling dry, and my saliva, thicker than molasses. I part my knees, praying he'll be content with this humiliation.

"Aren't you a good girl?" he asks, his right hand moving from the bed to my knee, then sliding across my thigh.

I tremble under his touch. "Jason?"

"Yes?"

"Please, stop." I don't remember ever begging anyone before. It doesn't feel good, but I have to.

"All right." He withdraws his hand. "Do it for me."

I blink in confusion.

"Touch yourself, and I won't."

My eyes widen.

"Come on, Nadia. Don't tell me you're unfamiliar with masturbation. It'd be pathetic."

I feel my cheeks burn under my skin. "The only pathetic thing is you having to resort to blackmail for a cheap thrill."

Jason is delighted. His hand moves to my face and I flinch, expecting a blow. It slows down and his fingertips reach out to graze my lower lip. "That mouth." He grins. "Hasn't it gotten you into enough trouble today?"

I want to bite his thumb off. Instead, I glare.

"Touch yourself or I will."

His thumb is still running along my lower lip, unsettling me. I must not have moved fast enough for him because he climbs on top of my bed and his left hand grips my hip.

A jolt freezes my skin under his touch, and I slap his hand away. "Don't! I...I'll do it."

I shove a hand into my pants and rub my clit manically, my face red with fury and embarrassment.

Still hovering right on top of me, Jason stares at my hand for what feels like an eternity. Then he throws his head back and laughs. "Gosh, you're terrible at this." He can't stop laughing. Could this situation get any more twisted? "I don't know whether you're ruining the show for my benefit or you just don't know what to do with your pussy. Either way, you had your chance, cupcake."

Without another warning, he grabs the fabric of my pajama shorts between my legs and rips them almost effortlessly.

I'm not wearing anything underneath.

I close my knees, but Jason pushes them apart. "Let me show you." Eyes staying on me, he moves one of his hands between my legs. I close them again, and this time, he lets me. He's exactly where he wants to be: right at the apex of my thighs.

His fingers slide over my flesh, softly, slowly, barely brushing against my clit as they pass over it. "That's it. Relax for me."

I glare at him. "Fuck you."

"Was that an invitation?"

I shut my mouth. If he was right about one thing today, it's that it's gotten me into enough trouble.

I'm determined to show no reaction to his ministrations. His fingers are light and teasing, and then his thumb presses on my clit and rubs it softly, slowly.

Oh.

*Oh.*

My eyes are wide, my heart racing.

He wasn't wrong about another point. I wasn't *trying* to masturbate well for him, but even by myself, I've never been very good at it with my fingers—I much prefer my vibrator.

I shouldn't have been surprised that Jason Alden knows *exactly* what to do with a pussy. I am though. Everything I know about him suggested he might have been the kind of guy to only concern himself with his pleasure.

I couldn't have been more mistaken. I don't want to let him do this to me, I'm as tense as I can be, and yet I feel tension build inside me, hotter and hotter as he patiently teases me. Of their own volition, my hips lift to meet his tantalizing touch. My throat is dry again, and I have a hard time breathing through my nose, so I pant.

One of Jason's fingers curves inside my folds, exploring my burning insides and my core tightens in response. I can only throw my head back and *feel.*

I don't recognize my voice. I don't recognize my body.

This, perhaps, is the worst thing that Jason's done to me. Owning my body as though he has a right to it. "Stop. Please, Jason, don't..."

"Shush, cupcake. You're almost there."

*Where?* I wanted to ask, lost and confused by what I was feeling. An overwhelming torrent without visible end, where nothing exists except the tense heat burning inside me. But I can't open my mouth again, not if I want to keep myself from screaming.

I see him unzip his pants with his free hand, and I tense, but somehow the motion brings his finger to a bundle of nerves so sensitive I lose all sense the moment he touches it. I throw my head back and scream.

Jason's mouth closes on mine, swallowing my sound. I know he's not kissing me as much as controlling me, but I'm too lost to fight any of this. His tongue dives into my mouth, coaxing mine to play. I don't response. I can control that, at least.

I feel him take my wrist and move my hand to something soft as velvet, yet hard. I glance down, but can't see much with him over me. Still, I'm not rendered stupid enough I fail to understand what he's done. He's put his dick in my grasp, and he expects me to please him. I'd rather fuck a cactus.

I let go, glaring at him.

Meeting his eyes is a mistake. He's entirely fixed on me, gaze boring deep into me, filled with a dangerous, cold glint. I've always assumed his eyes were brown but from this close, I can see I was mistaken. They're black.

"Now, don't be selfish, Nadia. This is supposed to work both ways. If you can't play nice, I'll just stick it in your pussy and come inside, rather than on it. Is that what you'd like, hm?"

I thrash against his hold, trying to kick him off me. I might as well have attempted to lift a whale, for all my effort accomplishes. I do manage to land a punch with the hand he's not holding, though. He removes his hand from my folds to hold my arm, then lifts the other one, and pins both of my hands over my head in one of his.

Jason licks his lower lip, taking a moment to look at me. He...likes this. He likes that I'm fighting him, that I don't want this. I can tell.

"Get off me!" Writhing is all I can manage, he has me pinned.

"Two words out of three. Not bad, cupcake." Jason lowers his hips to mine, and I freeze.

Now that he's hovering a little higher on top of me, I see his cock, huge, hard, and bare, mere inches from me. I try to close my legs, but his knees are keeping mine apart.

"Don't do this," I whisper, throat tight, eyes stinging with fury and helplessness.

"What, this?" He slides the head of his cock over my pussy. I'm ashamed that my sensitive folds can't help feeling pleasure at the friction.

His hips slowly sway forward and back, his cock

sliding against me. I clamp my mouth shut, determined not to show any form of appreciation, though my body can't help enjoying part of this.

Sick. He's sick, and so am I.

"Jason, please."

He just laughs. "I don't think you know what you're asking for, doll."

I think I prefer cupcake. He's treating me like a doll right now. His personal pleasure doll, without a will or agency.

*"I'm asking you to stop,"* I want to yell, but the moment I open my mouth, a moan is ripped out of my throat.

"Hmm. Are you going to be a good girl and do as you're told, then?" he asks me.

I. Hate. Him.

I nod helplessly.

Jason releases my hands and directs the right one back to his shaft.

I don't know how to do this. I glance up to him and immediately regret it. He's smirking, delighted with his victory. I'd rather look at his cock.

There's something obscene about seeing him still completely dressed in his blazer, shirt and tie, pants unzipped but not undone, while my legs are spread and bare.

I pump his dick with my fist.

Jason shifts closer to me, placing one hand back on my folds and grabbing a fistful of my hair with the other. He tugs at my ponytail until I sit up, and brings my mouth to his.

His fingers resume their attention, and my body responds, never caring that it's being pleasured by the devil.

I hate him. I hate him. I hate him. And for a moment, I hate myself too, because he feels so good.

"The tip. Move your hand higher, toward the tip. Grasp it tighter."

I do as I'm told. I've had enough *consequences* to last me a lifetime.

I didn't think it was possible, but the furnace inside me rages hotter, tighter, until I can't take it. Everything inside and around me explodes.

I fall back on the bed, limp and confused.

I thought I'd come before. I was wrong. If this was an orgasm, I've never experienced it until now.

When my senses return, I notice I've let go of his cock, and I look up at Jason, apprehension waking my frazzled mind.

He doesn't seem pissed this time. He's taken the matter in his own hands, so to speak, expertly rocking his fist around his shaft. I don't move. I don't make a sound. I just watch, my own core unexplainably stirring.

A translucent stream spurts out of him, landing on both the bed and me. Hot and viscous, the substance is everywhere, from my thighs to my stomach.

I make a face. "Ew."

Jason lifts an eyebrow. "Oh? I can make you swallow it next time if you'd rather avoid the mess."

*Next time.*

All the dormant fury slams back into me. I sit up and draw my hand back to slap his smug face. He grabs my wrist before I can hit him. "Violence is never the answer, sweet."

"You're telling me that, after *this*?"

Jason laughs. "Was I violent?"

My heart drops. I wish he had been. I wish he'd held me down and forced himself on me, so every part of me could have safely abhorred the experience. Instead, he made me participate. He made me choose. He made my body enjoy it.

"There will never be a *next* time. You're lucky if I don't report you to the police for this."

His chuckle makes me try to slap him with my other hand. He catches that one too, and moves my hands behind my back, before drawing me close to him. "But doll, you asked me to fill you with my cum." He bats his long lashes and pouts. "I suppose you could complain I only bathed you with it."

"You're disgusting."

"Right now, you are."

A different kind of fear clogs my brain. "Are you..." I feel myself blushing. "Are you clean?"

As far as sexual experiences go, this perverted version of it had been fairly safe, but he's touched my pussy with his cock, and some of his sperm might have gotten on my clit or something. I'm no expert. If he gave me an STD...

I feel even sicker than I have at any point so far today.

The question amuses him. "Squeaky. Are you?"

I don't dignify that with an answer.

I've only had sex once—a one-night stand last year that hadn't been anything to write home about—but I got checked after. He doesn't deserve to know that. He deserves crabs. I just hope he doesn't have it yet.

Deciding not to take his word for it, I make a mental note to get checked for STDs now and in six months.

"I need a shower. Don't be here when I come back."

I'm exhausted, and I can't take any more of Jason Alden tonight.

Scratch tonight. I can't take more of him for the rest of my life.

He lets me go—he's gotten what he wanted from me.

I remain under the stream of water until it runs cold, and then I stay there anyway.

I hate that Jason knows just how to touch me. Better than anyone I've chosen to make out with in the past. Better than *me*.

I'm exhausted and dreading another altercation, but when I come back out, my room is empty.

I'm surprised to see that my bedding has been changed. The covers are drawn tight, as tidily as when my mother makes it for me.

I loathe that part of me is grateful for this small kindness. In light of everything, no amount of thoughtfulness on his part ought to be acknowledged. He's a bastard, through and through.

As I fall asleep, dread coils inside me because I realize something.

He still has the leverage he held against me tonight. He could come back to my room every night and demand a repeat of tonight's obscenity.

*Now you belong to me.*

I hadn't believed him when he said it earlier.

Now I do.

That, more than anything, is terrifying.

# CHAPTER SIXTEEN

I wake with one certainty in mind. I need to switch schools.

I can see no other option where I retain a semblance of sanity—and freedom.

Jason marked me in several ways last night. He made me taste shame, fear, and, yes, pleasure, too. But worst of all, he made me comprehend one thing I'd never quite understood until him.

Power.

I knew the likes of Brooke and Yuki set the tone in the school. I knew they have better cars, shoes, and clothes than me, and more friends. Their wealth makes them popular.

Power is something else altogether. It's the ability to bring someone else to their knees and use them like a puppet.

Jason has power over me here in this school. If I go away, his power disappears. He won't be able to use my credentials, clone my phone, threaten my future. I can start over in the city.

We're still in September. Colleges may question my abrupt departure, but I can bullshit my way through an explanation. What I can't do is remain a pariah to my peers by day and become a whore under Jason's thumb at night for the rest of the year. I don't really like that word. It's disrespectful to sex workers. I like porn as much as the next teenager, who am I to judge the actors entertaining me? But it's appropriate for this situation. Jason used me like one.

I try to call my parents separately, then Uncle Lucius, all the while debating what I'll say once one of them answers. A pointless endeavor; none of them do. I send individual texts to all three of them, asking them to call me back as soon as they can.

I contemplate staying in the dorm for the day, but I'm too restless. Besides, my small, comfortable single room doesn't exactly feel like a safe haven anymore.

I skip breakfast, heading to school on autopilot.

"Hey, Nadia. I love your hair today," some girl tells me when she passes in front of my seat on the bus.

I glance up to her, frowning in confusion.

Other than Sophia, and the couple of outcasts sharing my table at the cafeteria, no one has said a word to me since the first day of school—unless you count insults. Not even Judith or Melina. We might have gotten along in the past, but the kings decreed me persona non grata, and they're legacies. They stick together.

I'm too stunned to answer, and I'm half waiting for a punchline, but she just keeps walking to join her friends a few rows back.

I don't remember doing anything to my hair. Did I even brush it? I know I washed it last night, just to have something to do under the shower. I glance at my dim reflection in the window of the bus, and I see that my mane's gathered on top of my head in a messy bun. There are a few strands falling out of it. Yep, I definitely didn't brush it. It doesn't look entirely terrible, so I decide the girl might have been sincere.

This morning is weird.

"Hey, Nadia!" one girl calls in the corridor, shooting me a radiant grin.

*What the fuck?* I'm fairly certain she tried to trip me last Thursday.

I get to my locker in a weary daze, waiting for the other shoe to drop, but the bizarre farce continues. A boy who I know is acing the class asks me if I need his notes in calculus. In Italian, after I answer one of the teacher's questions, some girl asks me if I've ever been to Italy. "Your accent is just so amazing!"

I don't respond to anyone—not the girls complimenting me all of a sudden, not the guys who tell me I'm "looking good, Reyes!" or offee to help me out on one thing or another. I trust this situation as much as I'd trust a cobra poised to strike.

By the time I make my way to AP lit, I'm tenser than I was at any point last week. The rules have changed, but I'm not dumb enough to think the game's over.

I'm already seated when I realize I probably should have skipped English. Now would be the perfect time to try to call my parents again.

I walked so fast to escape the bizarre alternative reality I've been thrust into, I'm the first in the classroom. I decide to just walk back out.

I only just got to my feet when Melina storms in, heading straight for me.

She grabs my forearm and speaks hurriedly. "You're here. Good. We don't have long to talk. Sit." Though she's small and dainty, she pulls me down with a force I hadn't expected. "Last Monday, the boys posted on the school wall, telling everyone to ice you. Today, they lifted the ban—for today only, you hear?" Words are rushing out so fast she could make a career out of auctioneering. "No one's supposed to tell you. I don't know what their game is, but I figured you'd want a heads-up." She glances over her shoulder, hearing footsteps approaching, and scampers to her seat.

I blink, taking in her speech.

By "the boys," she must mean Alden and Co., the four jerks. I'd known they were behind this mess, of course, but hearing that they organized my bullying like one would a school event was astonishing. And today, I wasn't a leper all of a sudden?

My jaw tightens.

I have to put up with this just a little while longer. I can get my parents to transfer me soon. I know it means I have to admit to the bullying, and I don't like that. They'll want to know who started it, they'll want to make a fuss with the school. I don't want any of that. All that matters is getting out of this hellhole.

I feel when Jason enters the room, although my eyes are glued to the doodle at the corner of my notebook. My entire being is aware of him on an animalistic level—I'm reduced to prey.

My eyes stay low, but I recognize his stride. I'm not surprised he takes the open seat to my right. Cain sits right behind him.

"Morning, doll."

*That name.*

"Don't be like that, Nadia. Your life is so much easier when you play nice, isn't it?"

My cuticles become fascinating. I'm not going to let him get to me. These are my last few days at Cross. My last few days with him. I can do this. I *can* do this.

Jason leans to me and pushes a wayward strand of hair behind my ear.

I can't do this.

## CHAPTER SEVENTEEN

The teacher isn't back from his interclass break so I don't have to justify myself. My notebook in one hand and throwing my bag on my shoulder, I just run out of there.

I don't have a clear destination in mind at first, but when I reach the entrance of the school, I pull my phone out of my skirt pocket and try to call everyone again.

Uncle Lucius answers on the second ring. "Dia," he says affectionately. "I got your message and put my phone on ring to catch you when you called again." Lucius has a perfectly normal New York accent. I don't know why people assume second-generation immigrants sound any different when they grew up here. His voice is warm and calming. "I didn't want to disturb you during your classes. Anything I can help you with, *tesoro*?"

Just a few words and I feel like crying.

I don't think I've cried at all since the start of this mess.

"I..." I don't know what to say. Suddenly, I'm not entirely sure of my course of action.

I remember Lucas's words. *"You're not a target. You're an Astrella."* I dismissed him at the time, but he's right. I am.

Dad might have been too busy with his work to have passed on the family motto to me, but Uncle Lucius did. I remember him teaching me how to ride my bike without training wheels. When I wanted to give up after my umpteenth fall, he told me, "You're an Astrella, *tesoro*. You're stronger than that."

Then there had been my first boxing lesson. I found the instructor—a professional he also hired to teach Lucas mixed martial arts—unnecessarily discouraging and demeaning. Of course I sucked on my first day, he didn't have to scream at me.

"He told me I'm weak," I snarled.

Uncle Lucius laughed. "Are you going to prove him right?"

He wasn't one to give up—on anything. He wouldn't stand where he was, dining with Fortune 500 CEOs and socialites every night, if folding had been in his nature.

I know that if I admit to being in over my head and ask to be pulled out of here, Uncle Lucius will have another school lined up by the end of the day, no questions asked.

I also suspect he'll be disappointed in me.

I think back to last night and rage immediately rises to the surface.

I was embarrassed. Embarrassed of being trapped, of losing, of being prey to Jason. I was also afraid of how far he intended to take it, but bottom line, my pride had been more hurt than anything else.

Jason had started a game and I was losing.

Astrellas didn't like losing.

"I was wondering when Lucas is coming back. I only saw him last Friday."

My uncle pauses on the other end of the line. "We're closing an important deal. Lucas has been pivotal for its completion, and I don't want him to miss out on it. He should be back more regularly starting next week, I promise."

I nod, then realize, dumbly, he can't see me. "All right, thank you, *zio*."

"Your mother let me know you came home this weekend. Will you be in town this week? We could do brunch."

I hop inside the bus back to the dorm. "Brunch sounds amazing. Sunday?"

"I'll arrange the time and send a car. I'm in the middle of a meeting—was there anything else, *tesoro*?"

I can't believe he answered me in the middle of a meeting. This morning's message must have freaked him out.

"No, that's it. Thank you."

I'm thanking him for unknowingly infusing

strength back into me, not for brunch, but he doesn't have to know.

I head straight to the administrative building. The receptionist seems frazzled and too busy for my request, but at my insistence, she buzzes Ms. Casey. I have to wait five minutes until the assistant calls me into her office.

"Ms. Reyes. I hope there were no more incidents." Her eyes size me up.

"None." None I'm going to report.

"Ah. Then why are you here during the school day?"

"Cramps," I blurt out. "I had to grab pain killers."

She nods, understanding. "I'll write you a note for your next class, but don't make a habit of being unprepared."

"While I passed in front of the building, I remembered I had to come see you. I was just wondering if you could help me with my schedule. I know you said I had to make my mind up last week about adding an elective, but the week flew by and I..." *had other concerns, like getting bullied by the entire school,* "forgot to pop by."

She smiles kindly. "I'll see what I can do."

That sounds encouraging. "There's no class I want to take during my free period at two," I say. "But I think I saw an architecture class at eleven? I could take that one, and move to two for English."

My master plan lets me avoid my one and only class with Jason.

Fingers flying on her keyboard, she frowns. "That's a regular English class, Nadia, not an advanced placement."

I shrug. "It shouldn't matter that much so long as I ace it, right?"

"If you intend to attend an art college, you may want to reconsider," Ms. Casey tells me. "How about history at two?"

History happens to be the one discipline I did consider last week, before forgetting about signing up. But that doesn't fix my Jason problem.

Then again, he doesn't do much to me in class. I nod. "Yeah, that sounds good. Can you squeeze me in?"

"I'll email Mr. Michaels, but it shouldn't be a problem, as the class is not full. I'll have an answer in your inbox by the end of the day, along with a list of the required materials. You might be able to get the book in the library."

"Thanks, Ms. Casey."

That's a loss, as far as my plan to get out from under Jason goes, but it's a win for my transcript. I shake her hand and get out.

On my way out, I see Brooke in the entry hall, waiting in front of the receptionist's desk in front of a small group of students.

Her mouth curls into a smirk when she sees me, and she smooths her dyed hair. She squints. "Who are you again? Oh, Nadia. I almost didn't recognize you without smoothie down your shirt."

Apparently, she didn't get the memo about my

being out of the naughty corner today, by order of the king.

That or she doesn't care.

Ignoring her, I make my way out of the building, but as I pass her, she tries to swipe my feet from under me with a kick.

I flip out.

Maybe because of the last week, maybe because of last night, or simple because it's Brooke, I lose it and let my fist fly. I punch the bitch right in the face, like I've wanted to for years, every time she insults her own sister, mocking her weight or demeaning her for her academic proficiency.

Brooke gasps, her hands covering her face, half sputtering, half crying. I see blood trickle from between her fingers. Alessandro might have been a dick of a teacher, but thanks to him, I have a mean right hook.

I should probably feel bad, but I don't. The only rain on my parade is the fact that this shit is going to get me in serious trouble now.

The receptionist rushes out of the restroom after hearing the commotion. She gasps when she takes in Brooke. "What happened!" Her eyes are wide.

Brooke immediately points at me. "Nadia punched me!"

*Guilty as charged.*

I won't get expelled for this, will I? Part of me wants to laugh. Here I am, setting out to stay in this school and fight against my bullies, and I might have bought myself a way out instead.

At least if they kick me out, it won't be me giving up.

"Brooke, you must be mistaken." I freeze as I hear a smooth, deep, calm voice.

I don't recognize it as well as Jason's, but I know it's one of the three others before I lift my eyes to see Maverick detach from the congregation behind Brooke, and smile pleasantly at the receptionist.

His green gaze is piercing, and everyone in the reception area turns to him. "I saw you fall, and Nadia here only tried to help you up. I get the confusion, it happened so fast, but Nadia's entirely innocent."

I'm baffled.

And suspicious. Why the *fuck* would *he* help me?

Jason might have declared me out of the ice box he'd shoved me in for today, but it still doesn't make sense that one of the four kings would lend me a hand.

Astonished and distraught, Brooke gapes at Maverick, her mouth opening and closing several times, making her look like a fish out of water.

The receptionist finally tears her eyes away from Maverick to turn to Brooke, waiting for her to either confirm or deny Maverick's version of the events.

Under Maverick's steel gaze, Brooke doesn't lower her head or show any sign of submitting to him. I have to give her that—the girl has balls.

Finally, though, she mumbles, "I must have been mistaken."

The receptionist nods. "Well, let's get you to the infirmary, dear. Thanks for helping, Nadia."

"You're welcome. I'll gladly help Brooke any time."

I'm pushing my luck, but I don't seem to care.

Maverick disguises a laugh in a cough.

I make my way out, walking toward the parking lot, when footsteps sound behind me. I glance over my shoulder, tensing when I see Maverick trailing me.

Time to see the price of his faux chivalry, I suppose. If he suggests anything gross, I'm cutting his balls off with my art scissors. Although, I love those scissors. It'd be a shame to have to replace them.

I don't stop, but I don't speed up either. His long strides bring him to me in no time.

"What do you want?" I finally ask.

"Were you in there to report Jason?" Maverick's voice is casual, almost bored.

Now I stop and turn to look at him. I wonder just how much he knows about what Jason did to me.

"How is that any of your business, asshole?"

He shrugs. "I'm simply curious. If you did, getting out of Cross isn't the worst idea." He snorts. "I'd actually book a flight out of the country if I were you."

It could have sounded like a threat, but Maverick makes it sounds like advice.

I study him, and remember that while Rowan was happy to start last week's hell with his smoothie, Cain delights in my misery, and Jason…is Jason, Maverick hasn't done anything to me. Not really.

Yet.

I settle for telling him the truth. I can't exactly pinpoint why, but my instincts tell me he could be an ally of sort amongst my enemies. At least he'd hesitate before signing my death warrant.

I'm being unnecessarily dramatic, but fuck, I've had a *day*. "Of course I didn't report Jason. I'm not dumb."

He nods. "Well, that remains to be seen. But smart call, Reyes. Keep up the good work."

He walks back to the reception hall.

What the hell?

# CHAPTER EIGHTEEN

I'm excused for my English period, and I have lunch after, which gives me enough time to drive to town and shop for supplies.

I'm not one for DIY, but a cute associate with green pixie hair and several nose piercings is happy to show me around the hardware store. I buy the strongest lock in the store, and she sells me the tools I need to install it. Jason's never getting back into my room uninvited.

Which means he's never getting back into my room. I don't intend to invite him. Ever.

On my way back to the car, I pass a taco stand, and all of a sudden I feel so faint I almost keel over. My neglected stomach howls in desperation.

Tempting as the scent had been, I'd chucked out Jason's burger last night, and I hadn't felt like eating at breakfast, so the last thing I'd ingested was a granola bar what felt like a lifetime ago.

It's not twelve yet, a little too early for lunch,

but there's a small line in front of the hole-in-the-wall stand. Some guy wearing an ill-fitting suit is first in line, followed by two gossiping old ladies.

Jesus, the smell is driving me *insane*.

One of the biddies turns to me, eyeing me up and down. "Shouldn't you be at school, young lady?"

"In my day, no one left in the middle of our classes to do god knows what," the other one is quick to add.

The first shakes her head. "Hush, now, Cynthia—Teddy told me all about it. They have 'free periods' sometimes." To me, she says, "You look like the good sort, dear. I'm sure you're not skipping."

Well, she'd be wrong.

I smile awkwardly. "Thanks?"

"She looks uppity," Cynthia grumbles. "That's the big, fancy school up the road's uniform, isn't it? The ones who bought the lake."

Cynthia glares at me like I'm personally responsible for the purchase of said lake, made decades before my birth. Even they don't look old enough to have been alive back when the purchases were made.

"And in doing so, they made your family and mine quite comfortable," the kinder one reminds her. She rolls her eyes. "Our families used to own lake houses where your school was built. There's a painting of Cynthia's on her mantelpiece."

"Best view in town," Cynthia announced proudly. "And now we can't see it—we can't share it with our grandchildren. My poor Teddy will never swim in the lake."

"Isn't there another lake a couple of miles south?" I ask. I'd run around there a few times with the track team.

Cynthia shrugs. "Not as pretty."

"Next!" the taco guy calls.

The old ladies place their order, then grumpy old Cynthia turns to me. "Well, what will it be?"

I blink. Up until this moment, I thought she hated my guts by default but apparently, Cynthia wants to buy me lunch. "Oh, I can get my own."

"Indulge an old lady," Cynthia's friend says, patting my hand.

"I'm going to order a lot," I admit.

Cynthia eyes me up and down. "Good. All skin and bones, you are. You have to get a little padding, yes? You're not a vegetarian, are you?" Before I can answer, she turns to the guy still waiting for the rest of our order. "Two of the special for the uppity girl."

"Coming right up, Cyn."

He starts preparing our food, and my stomach grumbles audibly as I see him mix fresh ingredients, cooking marinated meat and veggies right before my eyes. Oh, this is going to be good. So good.

Our food's ready within minutes and Cynthia hands me two fresh tortillas filled to the brim. I could cry.

I stand there awkwardly, wondering if they want me to eat with them, but the old ladies wave as they walk away and tell me to "get my skinny self back to school."

Which I do, while eating the best tacos I've ever had. My mother would probably pout if I admit it to her, but they're just *so* much better than hers. Unless I'm just starving.

I get back toward the start of my lunch hour, so I use the time to install the door lock. A huge weight lifts from my shoulders.

When my mother calls me back around twelve thirty, I can honestly tell her I'm fine. "I just wanted to let you know I'll be home this weekend, too."

She pauses on the other end. "Is everything all right, Dia? You rarely came back on weekends last year."

The best lies stay close to the truth. "This year isn't as much fun. Besides, I told Uncle Lucius I'd meet him for brunch Sunday."

"All right." She's easily convinced. "I'll clear my Saturday this time, yes? We can go shopping. My treat."

I try not to wince.

I like shopping as much as the next girl, and I could use a couple of things.

My mother? She *loves* it. She keeps going even when our arms are full of bags and our feet, heavier than after a five-mile run. And she tends to do it in four-inch heels, too. If we didn't look so much alike, I'd question whether we're related. I'd question whether she's human, for that matter.

For all that, I like spending time with my mom, so I say, "Sure."

"Do you want me to check with Sandro to see if he has a shift for you at the restaurant?"

I consider saying yes, but after shopping with her, the last thing I'll want would be carrying trays of drinks. "Not this weekend. If we're doing brunch, I don't want to go to bed too late Saturday."

We hang up.

I notice Dad left a message to check if he can help with anything. I shoot him a quick text to let him know about the weekend.

Once that's done, I remain in my bedroom, sitting back on my bed for a few seconds. Without anything to distract me, memories from last night flash through my mind. His hands. His tongue. Jason pinning me down under him.

I need to decorate. Change everything about this place to make it mine, and wipe Jason away from my space.

Somehow.

# CHAPTER NINETEEN

## Jace

I lean back in my chair, eyes closed, tuning out the irritating cacophony around me. I can't stand lunchtime at Cross. Our first few years, we sat with the rest of the football team and the cheer team, but one day last year, I'd gotten up and gone to the next table to our right. Some guys I didn't know vacated it and I claimed it. Cain followed without question—a habit of his.

Rowan bitched, naturally, but he came, too, and where Rowan goes, Maverick follows.

It's funny that everyone thinks the four of us are such great friends. I can't stand Rowan. He'd happily run me over with his stupidass Jeep if murdering me wouldn't cost him money.

We're business partners, end of discussion.

Cain imprinted on me like a puppy when we were kids. I can't say I mind. I like dogs. They're blindly loyal—and blindness is the only way to be loyal to me.

Rowan is Cain's half brother, a fact a rare few individuals are aware of, and the only reason why the four of us were pushed together. We remained a unit because, as little as I actually like any of them, I respect them.

Cain's a genius—having one of those in my pocket has come in handy more times than I can count. Rowan's moral compass is more skewed than mine, which in itself is an achievement. I can be cold, and perhaps cruel, to achieve my aim. Rowan's cruel for the hell of it. And Maverick has what none of the rest of us can boast of: a heart. That, too, occasionally has its uses. Mav made it his life's mission to keep Rowan in check. Why, I'm not sure. Maybe Rowan's good at sucking his dick—who knows.

"Oh, for fuck's sake, lighten up a little, bitch." I don't have to open my eyes to know Rowan's talking to me. He's relatively civil toward the rest of the group. "Your karma's messing with the taste of my pizza. What's got your panties in a twist?"

Cain answers for me. "She skipped English." He doesn't have to elucidate on the *she*.

Now I open my eyes, shooting him a pointed glare.

Cain grins, unapologetic. "What? You've been tetchy since then."

"Maybe I have a headache."

"Or maybe you need to get it over with and fuck her," Rowan counters.

My headache's name is Rowan.

He's trying to get on my nerves, but I won't take the bait.

I could have had Nadia under me, over me, any which way, days ago. Years ago, if I'd known she was here, within reach.

Fire and ice stab my chest, like they always do when I think back to the first time I saw her. The first time I touched her.

She's forgotten by now, no doubt. I haven't.

I can't.

"He doesn't want to fuck her," Maverick informs Rowan. "He wants to own her."

I glance at the guy, surprised at his uncharacteristically accurate guess. Out of the three of them, Mav is the most different from me. I don't mind the guy, but I barely understand him and his desire to be a fucking saint or something. Maybe it's because of his upbringing, in his sickeningly sweet, picture-perfect family. I get a toothache every time I'm in the Eaton household.

As far as Heritage families go, I could have done worse. My parents make time for me. They aren't dead, like Rowan's, or messed up like Cain's. That said, my upbringing was nothing like Maverick's.

Mine included darkness, fear, and blood—some of it, on my hands.

He's right though. I'm not going to all this effort just to screw Nadia.

"Oh." Rowan stares at me, stunned, then makes a face. "Why her?"

*Why, indeed.*

I glance at Cain. If he says a word, I'll shove his face into the nearest wall. Wisely, he doesn't.

Rowan rolls his eyes. "All right, whatever, keep your secrets." He finishes his pizza in a few bites. "How can I help?"

I hold his gaze, scrutinizing his expression. What's his game here? I can't make sense of it, but he has an agenda. Everyone does. Besides, I've never heard him offer to help anyone as long as I've known him—which is as long as I've been able to walk.

Rowan snorts. "You know, not all of us are calculating assholes." His grin is quick to disappear. "If you're playing for keeps, it's Heritage business. I'm in. I'd like to think you'd do the same for me if I found someone outside the club."

"Hmm." He seems sincere. Not that it matters. I don't trust him. I don't trust anyone who hasn't proven themself to me.

Which is highly unfortunate for Nadia. I need to trust her.

Which means I need to test her.

"I'll pass on the help. Stay away."

She's mine to torment.

# CHAPTER TWENTY

Gym has been the worst class by far, because the teacher is such a dick, until I walk into my history class at two in the afternoon.

Ms. Casey emailed me that the teacher okayed my late enrollment, so I go. Then I regret it.

*You've got to be fucking kidding me.*

All four guys are seated together toward the back. I'm too stunned to move.

Maybe it's not too late to drop the subject. Right?

I imagine Ms. Casey's expression if I walk into her office and ask for another change, and I drag my feet inside, eyes still on them, because not watching predators in my vicinity would be stupid.

They haven't noticed me yet. Maverick and Rowan chat together, Cain's playing on his phone and Jason's reading some book. It looks like fiction.

I frown, surprised. He doesn't strike me like a reader, somehow, but there he is.

I scan the room for a free seat far, far away from the quartet.

"Nadia!" Sophia waves her hand from the second row, grinning broadly at me.

I would have killed for her not to call attention to me. Now all the assholes stare at me. I see Rowan grin.

I turn to join Sophia—there's a free seat right behind her.

"You signed up for history?"

I shrug. "I had a free period, and I certainly wasn't going to take another year of chemistry."

She laughs, knowing how terrible I am at most sciences. "Hey, where were you at lunchtime, by the way?"

Mr. Michaels walks in in time to spare me needing to answer.

At least our class doesn't seem boring. As Ms. Casey said, not a lot of seniors take history for a fourth year. We've all already studied the usual. Mr. Michaels goes in depth about recent history—the 1900s. Most teachers don't feel comfortable reminding us how recently women became able to vote, how just in our grandparents' time, interracial couples couldn't get married—that sort of thing. Mr. Michaels has no such issue.

I try to concentrate and take notes, but with the eyes I imagine burning into my back, that's not an easy feat. At least I can borrow Sophia's notes if mine don't make sense.

When the bell rings, I shove my notes into my bag and rush out of the room.

"Wait!" Sophia calls.

I freeze, darting a glance at the back of the room.

Jason's staring right at me, eyes dancing with amusement.

*Fuck.*

Sophia's far too slow, taking her time to organize her bag.

"I've barely seen you since school started," she bemoans. "I'm so annoyed they changed our room arrangements. It's not the same without you."

I have to admit, I feel a little guilty, because, well, I haven't missed her all that much. I haven't really had time to deal with anyone else's drama, given what's been going on with me.

"I haven't even seen your tattoo yet!" She pouts.

"Tattoo," Jason echoes from far, far too close.

I practically jump when I realize he's standing next to me.

"How come I haven't seen it either, doll?"

I want to punch him. "Go fuck a cactus, asshole."

He tilts his head back. "Now, that wasn't very polite, Nadia. Don't you like it when things are friendly between us?" He leans against the nearest desk.

"We're not friends, Jason."

He takes a moment to think it through. "I suppose not. Fuck buddies, then."

I'm practically shaking with fury. "Stay away from me."

Sophia's barely zipped her bag when I grab her elbow and pull her out of the room.

I'm walking so fast I'm practically running, and hear Sophia panting a foot behind me. "Wait, Nadia!" She pulls her arm free, and bends down to catch her breath. "I'm going to the other side of the building."

*Oh.*

Right, I have art and she has her AP calculus torture.

"Sorry. I just had to get out of there. Jason is..."

Her eyes widened. "Why did he say that, that you're fuck buddies? Did you and Jason freaking Alden—"

"No," I interrupt. "There's no me and Jason. Not in this universe. He's just taken to getting on my nerves for kicks."

That sounds fake even to my own ears after what he said, and Sophia cocks an eyebrow, clearly not buying it.

The second warning bell rings, urging us to get to class. Sophia winces. "I have to run. Later! Tell me *everything.*"

Right. Just as soon as pigs soar the skies and unicorns gallop down Fifth Avenue.

# CHAPTER TWENTY-ONE

Art class is my one solace, the only moment I can have some peace in this school.

Our teacher makes us build whatever comes to mind with blocks of styrofoam for the first thirty minutes. I let my hands do the thinking for me, cutting up, gluing, and putting together something until I see a tree with a cute little house perched toward the top. Mr. Weir walks from workbench to workbench, silently judging our work and scribbling notes on his iPad.

He glances at my piece before moving along without comment.

Weir's a hardass. Tall and impossibly lean, he mostly feeds on the tears of his students by the looks of it. If Van Gogh had crawled out of his grave and painted *The Starry Night* right before his eyes, he would probably just nod, and give him a B- for his trouble.

I don't take it personally. In the last two years, he's improved my outlook as well as my techniques. I used to think I just wanted to draw and paint a little, because that's what I knew. Making us use various materials for short projects like the silly treehouse had opened my mind up to a lot more. Now I prefer sculpting. I love mixing clay and metal, assembling old and new in some weird, alternative art that's all my own. The biggest change in me is that now I realize that in a year, or a month, or a decade, I could take to blowing glass or assembling bottle caps.

"You will receive the grades for today's assignment on your online portal," he announced. "Now, proceed to your main project."

Every semester, we're graded on short daily projects, but also on one continuous piece we work on during the second half of each class.

Weir's helpful, so long as you have skin thick enough to take his harsh criticism. When he looks at my work, he says, "You've been building this up for one week and your structure's integrity is already questionable, Ms. Reyes. Whatever you're doing, it's likely to flatten like a pancake."

I blush, embarrassed, mostly because I see where he's coming from. The metallic base with four upright spikes is already holding the weight of a ceramic disc and I plan to add much, much more, including clay and steel scraps. If I want to make sure my sculpture will hold, I need to use stronger stabilizers. I should have thought of it myself, but well, I don't exactly start out with a straightforward idea of where things are going.

It's not too late to change the spikes holding the weight of the disc. I spend the rest of the hour heating the clay and welding metal twigs. Art is my last class of the day—the swimming club meets later—and Weir lets his AP students stay as long as we need while he grades art history papers in his adjacent office. I finish my work and wash up at the sink.

I like to linger in order to avoid the bulk of the crowd heading back to the dorm from the school.

I'm the only one riding on the bus today. The quiet's nice. Knowing that the football team is still practicing doesn't hurt, either. Their Majesties don't ever ride the bus with the plebes, of course; they have drivers to chauffeur them to and from Glass. But for a couple of hours, I'm guaranteed to not have to deal with any of them. Pierson's making them run laps in the rain.

I've managed to accumulate some homework over the last few days. I normally keep on top of it, especially so early in the year, but my personal drama has affected my focus. I catch up on the class I missed and the work I need to get done before my swimming club meets. After getting showered and dressed, I reluctantly make my way to the common room where breakfast and dinner are served in the dorm.

It's more informal than the lunch at the cafeteria—instead of rows of identical tables that can seat six, there's a huge banquet table on the farthest wall. The rest of the room's cozy, with low coffee tables, sofas, and armchairs scattered near the windows and the large fireplace.

The food changes every day, but there's usually a selection of stews, soups, freshly baked rolls, meat cuts, fish, and salads. The evening chef's better than the cafeteria team.

I serve myself a generous helping of chorizo and sweet potato stew, grab a roll, and move to a couple of armchairs. Sophia wasn't here yet, but I'd come prepared, armed with a book and my headphones.

I lift my head when I see someone plop down on the armchair in front of mine, fully expecting Sophia, but it's a guy I had chemistry with last year. I've never spoken to him and can't remember his name. With dark locks and green eyes, tall and well built, some might think of him as cute, I suppose. His leer and his smirk make me want to slap his face, and wash my hands right after.

"How is it going, Nadia?"

I lift an eyebrow, and then point to my headphones, using them as an excuse.

He lifts his hands to his ears and gestures like a Neanderthal, motioning for me to remove them, like the thought could never have crossed my mind without his help. I consider just flipping him off, but it occurs to me that I may be rid of this idiot faster if I comply.

I sigh, lower the device, and ask, "What do you want?"

He grins at his victory, shuffling closer. "Hey. I thought we could hang, you know. There's a party at the lake tonight."

I nearly roll my eyes. "I don't even know your name."

"Rob. Rob Parry. So, how about it?"

"Pass." I redirect my attention to my book. "My friend's coming, move away, please."

The guy glowers at me. "Whoa. You're full of yourself, aren't you? No wonder the legacies want to put you in your place, bitch."

"Lashing out after rejection. That's *so* evolved of you." This time, I do roll my eyes. "Move, or I'll make you move, Rob Rob Parry."

In my old school in New York, kids used to be treated like criminals, always suspected, punished at the first infraction. This place couldn't be any more different. The security is tight at the gates, but we're more or less left to our own devices within the school. We're supervised, but from a distance. Our overseers only interfere if a huge fight breaks out, which almost never happens.

Still, when I lift my hand and wave to the short, stout woman in uniform pacing along the wall, she can't exactly ignore me.

Watching her walk toward us, Rob Rob gets up and leaves.

I put my headphones back on and eat the rest of my food.

I finish before Sophia arrives.

Digging my phone out of my pocket, I check if she sent me a message. Nothing.

I'm done, and I don't want to loiter with the people gathered here, so I head back to my room.

It's past ten when Sophia texts me to mention her new friend Yuki invited her down to the lake for dinner. Which is just fine. I would have preferred an advance warning, as we usually eat together, but there's no point in getting upset. I make a mental note not to take her company for granted in the future, and I try to tell myself that doesn't hurt.

Things have changed between us since the beginning of the year. I don't know if I'm distant because of everything going on with me, or if she's the one who stepped away first. What's clear is that our table should stop calling us the "twinset". We're no longer attached at the hip, that's for sure. Part of me doesn't entirely mind.

The last couple of years, she and I stuck together because I didn't quite fit in with the others around me, and because her sister was causing trouble for her. This year, I don't have the energy to fight her battles, and she doesn't have the time to provide company for me, so I suppose neither of us is getting much from our relationship.

I lock my door behind me and climb into bed with a book. Just as I turn the lamp off a couple of hours later, my eyes catch a flash of light outside the window. I can't remember the last time I've seen a shooting star. At Cross and Roses, the night sky has always been infinitely clearer than in New York City—we can actually see the stars here.

I'm not superstitious at all. It feels childish, but I don't care. I make a damn wish. I'm that desperate.

## CHAPTER TWENTY-TWO

I'd like to say things improved for me from there, but my day-to-day life is pretty miserable for the next three weeks. Shooting stars are bullshit. Go figure. Next, someone is going to tell me Santa doesn't exist.

Just as Milena warned, the student body only left me alone for one awkward, paranoia-inducing day. After that, the girls who complimented my hair or my lipstick are back to belittling me, or worse. Sophia's busy with her new legacy friends, so I barely get to see her outside of my Italian class. She rarely eats at our old table. I gradually come to terms with that, though it certainly doesn't help my sense of isolation in this gilded prison.

When I'm restless in the afternoons, after art and before the swimming club, I run, which is a great way of emptying my mind of concerns. If nothing else, it allows me to stay away from everyone else. And thanks to the exertion, I'm exhausted every night and I can crash despite my shifting anxiety.

When I don't work out hard enough to crash, I lay awake wondering what kind of abuse I can expect the next day. Will it be a rumor about me and some guys? According to current gossip, I've pretty much fucked the entire soccer and basketball teams. The only jocks who haven't made such a claim yet are the members of the football team.

Or maybe they'll suggest I only get straight As in classes taught by men because I suck them off for better grades. Which is majorly gross. The English professor might be relatively young and easy on the eyes, but *ew*. And don't even get me started on the wrinkly, old, rail-thin art teacher. I heard Brooke say I also fucked someone for my tuition, because how could a cook's daughter afford a place at Cross and Roses?

Then there's the straightforward physical abuse. I've been pushed into a cupboard and locked away until a maintenance guy found me at night. I've been tripped, stolen from, accused of stealing, yelled at, and Martin Lee grabbed my breasts yesterday at lunch. I kneed him in the junk, so hopefully he learned his lesson. I doubt it though. I saw the glint in his eyes—I'm fairly certain that if we hadn't been in the cafeteria, with supervisors and tons of witnesses, he wouldn't have dropped it.

I see Their Majesties every day. They never directly interact with me, letting the rabble do their dirty work for them. Every day, *he* looks at me, staring at me intently, until he's certain I get his silent message. *"You could end this. Yield and you'll be rewarded."*

Jason hasn't tried to come to my room—that I know of. The first few days, I expected my door to squeak or rattle, but no one tried the handle. I don't know what game he's playing, but I know I'm not giving in.

The last gasp of summer gives way to fall, my favorite season, especially upstate where I actually get to enjoy the landscape. Three more seasons. I can endure that much in this place. The solitude is bearable and helps my focus. I've never had better grades. I don't even do half bad in calculus. That only feeds the rumors about my sleeping my way through my instructors, but it's so ridiculous I'm not even mad about it.

On sunny days, when I'm lucky, I get to hang out with Cat outside the U in the courtyard. I call him Cat because he looks well fed, and only has a nameless collar with a phone number. I'm certain he has an actual name. Choosing another one feels rude.

The second Friday of October, I walk into the cafeteria and the first thing I notice is my cousin.

As Uncle Lucius promised, Lucas came back to school periodically beginning a couple of weeks ago. We've hung out, and we do share three classes, but Lucas has his own life, his own friends—most of whom delight in torturing me when he's not around.

He's seated at the jocks' tables—the one Their Majesties have boycotted for about a year. The other tables in the cafeteria sit six to eight students, but they've put three tables together in order to accommodate the baseball, football, and soccer teams, plus their cheerleaders. Lucas plays soccer. He generally makes sure he attends every game, and the coach deals with his frequent absences because he's just that good.

Lucas waves me over when he spots me, but I just sigh quietly. He should know better. I never go into the details of my ostracism with Lucas, but he's aware that most of the school is giving me a hard time, and he's not dumb enough to not realize that that sort of bullshit always starts with the popular crowd, his so-called friends.

At my request, he's left my issue with the rest of the school alone, as far as I can tell. The bullying seems to dampen considerably on days when he attends school, because while not everyone is aware of the fact that we're related, people know we're friends. One sharp glance from him and whoever's about to approach me takes seven steps back. He doesn't try to force people into playing nice with me, thank fuck. If he did, the situation would get out of hand on days when he's not around.

I sit at my usual table, sans Sophia. She's taken to sitting with Yuki and the rest of the It girls of Cross—Manon Montgomery, Jacqueline Billington, Judith, and even Brooke. Though she looks like she's sucking on a lemon every time they interact, her older sister leaves her alone now. Maybe because of Yuki's protection. Maybe because Sophia looks radiant and confident these days. She wears her uniform fitted to her size, accentuating her killer curves. She's also learned to apply makeup. She used to cake it over her skin, using the wrong colors and too many layers. I tried to help her out but she got sensitive when I said anything. "Not everyone has perfect, flawless skin, Nadia. I need more foundation."

I suppose she listens to Yuki's advice. I try to be happy for her, but part of me hates that we drifted so far apart this year. Especially since deep down, I can't help thinking that this was purposeful. I could swear our distance is Jason's doing. A move to further weaken and isolate me. Why else would *Yuki*, the legacy queen, suddenly pay attention to my best friend? I feel wicked for thinking that way. There are plenty of reasons to find Sophia interesting. She's smart, a little crazy but in a fun way, she loves good music and older movies—the three-hour pepla where everyone wears leather sandals. I just can't shake the notion that it was all to piss me off because of the timing. Yuki never cared about Sophia until Jason decided I should suffer.

"Eww." Willow makes a face. "Melon. Why do they hide melon in fruit salads?" She pushes her bowl away, thoroughly disgusted.

I spend more time with the redhead I met a month ago than with Sophia these days. Willow's cool. She's likely to become our valedictorian—Sophia's *good*, but she's not taking as many AP classes, so she'll probably make salutatorian.

Right after her classes, Willow hurries out of Cross to her job at a deli in town. Making friends with a waitress? Genius. She shares leftovers at least once a week at lunch. She also remains at school on weekends to work for two full days. I don't know her story—we're not that close—but she doesn't mind admitting that she needs the money. Coming from a working-class family, I like working to make my own pocket money, and to save for college. Willow says she's actually poor. Her brain got her into this school, but she still needs to save up to keep a roof over her head.

I asked about her parents once. After the look she shot me, I didn't ask again.

"Wanna swap?" I offer, pushing my dessert to her.

I picked a brownie, because I'm not a fool. Besides, between the swimming and my runs through the school grounds, I totally can have as many brownies as I'd like.

Willow hesitates. "I already tried mine."

I shrug. "You bring us bagels all the time. Have at it."

She doesn't ask twice, moving the dessert to her tray and attacking it with gusto. She always eats like that; like the food in front of her could be her last meal.

I don't try her fruit salad. Melon *is* kind of gross, especially out of season.

I'm waiting for Willow to finish when I sense him before hearing or seeing him.

Jason.

He drags the metallic feet of the chair next to mine over the tiled floor and sits, like it's the most natural thing in the world.

I don't acknowledge his presence, stiff and suddenly cold. I want to get up and go, but again, my pride prevents me from showing any weakness in front of him.

"Nadia," he says. "Burdon, Elisa," he greets the two other friends left at our table by name, before glancing at Willow appreciatively. She's very pretty. I want to kick Jason's chair. "And...I think we're in AP calculus together? I'm Jason."

"We are," Willow replies, without giving him her name.

I could cheer.

Jason turns back to me. "I know you usually stay in the city over the weekend, but please make an exception next week. We're having a get-together at Glass for Halloween. You should come."

I laugh in his face, getting to my feet. "I'll see you tomorrow, guys," I tell the people I eat with, ignoring the asshole.

Which may not be the wisest course of action, but as it so happens, I don't care.

## CHAPTER TWENTY-THREE

My primary AP art project is really starting to come together. I had no clue what I was going for when I started, but a month into it, I see her—a Gorgon, both beautiful and monstruous, lovingly whispering to her snakes of metal and clay. Though she's wounded, she doesn't seem to care. I suppose she's used to it.

Her face is almost finished. Although I have a lot of definition work to do later, I'm well on track to finish by the end of the semester when we get graded.

Footsteps sound, soft against the floor, but it's enough to break me out of the spell art tends to weave on me. Mr. Weir nods when he looks at my work. I know getting a nod from him isn't an everyday occurrence.

"It's been some time I since I've seen Greek

mythology in this classroom. Is that Medusa, Nadia?"

I shook my head. "Everyone knows Medusa's story. This is Stheno, one of her immortal sisters. They were cursed at the same time. Stheno's the big sister. I like portraying her with wounds, but ignoring them and keeping on living. She still finds it in herself to be kind to those who matter to her. Even though they're monsters. She's strong, confident. She's killed twice as many men as both of her sisters combined, and no hero got the best of her."

I'm surprised to hear my teacher laugh. "Is that admiration I hear?"

I feel my cheeks heat. I suppose I've shown quite a bit of enthusiasm for murder. "Well, you know. They only murdered so-called heroes who came to fight them on their territory. Nowadays, we would basically call it self-defense."

Mr. Weir lifts a placating hand. "I remember being young. In my high school days, I would have turned half the school to stone if I could. Don't worry, I'm not here to judge your feelings. Just your expression of them. It's good work."

The teacher moves along, and I get back to the task, grinning. I don't want to be arrogant, but I think I'm going to get an A for sure on this one. *Tisch, here I come...*

I take my empty crate and go pick up more material in the storage room next door.

There was always a box with random scraps of metal, but unless I'm very much mistaken, it has a much bigger selection now—torn pieces of steel that look like ominous spears, smooth, bent metal that would do a wonderful cheekbone peeking out of Stheno's clay skin. As I'm working on the face now, I take the steel bone and some more clay.

I'm smiling when I come back into the room. That doesn't last.

Mr. Weir's thin face is tight with cold fury as he speaks to one of the students—Marie Jones. She keeps her eyes downcast under the chastising. The rest of the class is gathered around them, their faces showing various ranges of shocked and appalled.

I barely even see them. I can't hear a word anyone is saying.

My eyes are on my work station.

The sculpture I've worked on for the last five weeks has been smashed on the floor. Hard. All of the clay is in pieces.

I can't move. I can't talk. I can only stare in horror. It feels like losing a piece of me.

This is no accident. Supported as it was, my work could have handled a fall. Some shards of metal have been dislodged too. It was *thrown* with enough force to ensure its complete destruction.

Nothing my peers have ever done to me hurt this way. Nothing.

Mr. Weir sees me, straightens up, and sighs before taking a step towards me. "I'm so sorry, Nadia, there has been an incident. Now, I've seen your work until now—I can grade on that with no penalty." His usually slow and stern speech is rushed and uncertain. "If you'd like an extension, that's also possible. Or I can give you leave to work on your project outside of school in case you'd like to finish it."

"I..." My voice sounds all wrong, weak and congested. No wonder. My throat is dry. I clear it before speaking again. "I need some air."

I head out of doors. I don't think he calls me back, but I wouldn't have stopped either way. Halfway to the exit, I start running. The walls feel like they're closing around me. I can't breathe. I can't think.

At the courtyard, I come to a sudden halt, and not because of the cold rain pouring on the cobblestones.

He's here. Jason. He's wearing his ridiculous black and red letterman jacket.

Of course he's here.

I'm fucking miserable, and he wouldn't want to miss that. I bet the bitch texted him the moment she obliterated my work.

He sees me and frowns. "Nadia. Are you okay?"

He must be fucking joking.

I cross the space separating us, each step determined, my fingers curled into fists, my nails digging into my palms.

I punch him, or I would've, but he catches my fist with a chuckle.

"Oh, Nadia, darling."

Fury singes my entire body, and I try again and again to hit him. He wanted a war; now he's getting it. It's on him. He deflects my blows with ease, still laughing, acting like this is some kind of game.

It's not a game. This is my life he's ruining for his entertainment. I yell as I let all of my rage, frustration, fear, and sadness out with each swing. They get weaker as I tire and as the rain drenches my blazer. Jason doesn't even bother to evade or block a couple of pathetic bitch slaps against his chest. Then he catches both of my hands and locks me in a twisted embrace, my arms tight to my sides.

I refuse to hug him back, but to my shame, confusion, and anger, I cry against his chest. I can't help it. It's all too much.

Until now, the bullying hasn't really bothered me. Or maybe it did and today was the last straw. I can't tell.

I think today crossed the line because I care about my art. This class had felt like a sanctuary, and now that's also tainted.

Jason says nothing, one of his hands caressing my back in a slow, comforting rhythm. I soak it up. I feel incredibly stupid for crying on him and accepting this comfort when all of my issues are basically his fault.

The rain freezes my hair, my clothes, and my bones, yet somehow, I'm not cold inside.

He's my enemy.

He's also all I have right now and I *need* someone.

"I hate you," I tell him, just in case he misunderstands the situation.

This changes nothing.

"I know."

Even though I know the answer, I ask the pointless question anyhow. "Will you leave me alone? Please."

He says nothing at first. When his reply comes, it's slightly unexpected. "I can't."

# CHAPTER TWENTY-FOUR

I play and replay the events of Friday all night and most of Saturday.

It's no longer about the sculpture. I put in a lot of work on it, sure, but there's no point crying over spilled milk—or wrecked clay. I might have worked on it for five weeks, but only for half an hour five days a week—that's only about a dozen hours of work. I can make up for it.

I spend most of the day working on another piece that'll do nicely for my final project. It needs another day or two, given how long clay takes to set, but I'll get it done in plenty of time now that Mr. Weir's allowed me to work on it outside of class.

What won't leave my mind is how I let Jason *hug* me.

*Ugh. Kill me now.*

I put it down to shock. Or insanity.

I spend an unhealthy amount of time thinking about his answer to me.

*"I can't."* Not "I don't want to, torturing you is too much fun." *"I can't."*

Jason is honest, hopelessly so, and he always chooses his words with care. He thought about it for a good long while before replying, too. He meant it.

*"I can't."*

I want to know what he means. I...need to. He's making my life a living hell. The least he can do is tell me why.

It shouldn't matter. No reason he might have would be valid. He's a horrible guy, that's it.

I can't stop thinking about it nonetheless.

"Dia, darling?" My mother knocks at my door, and opens it before I invite her in. "You've been cooped up in here working all day. Don't you want to stretch your legs?"

I grin and lift my eyebrows. "By that, I suppose you mean go shopping with you?"

She nods furiously. "There's a sale I don't want to miss at Saks, sweetie. Tell me you'll come with me."

She's nothing if not predictable. Saks isn't my scene, but I go along.

We've made Saturday afternoon shopping trips a new tradition since the start of the year, I suppose. I'm still uncomfortable seeing my mother spend so much money on stuff she doesn't actually need when she doesn't work, while Dad seems to live at the restaurant, but the chat we had at the start of the year has put things in perspective. They're adults. If Dad doesn't want her money, she can't make him take it. Their relationship doesn't seem particularly healthy—or loving—to me, but what do I know? At least they never seem to fight.

Mom tries on a dozen of pairs of shoes, modeling them for me. Looking at her long, strong legs and the way she effortlessly sways in her four-inch heels, she looks every bit the ballet dancer.

"Mom, have you ever thought about going back to performing?" She teaches a few ballet classes at a local school, but I've seen her dance. She could still be out there touring the world if she wanted to.

She snorts. "I'm a bit too old for professional ballet, sweetie."

I have a hard time believing it. Mom had me when she was twenty-two. She'd been dancing professionally since she was sixteen, and she was already the prima ballerina of a world-renowned company.

My incredulity must have shown on my face, because she continues. "Most dancers retire in their mid-thirties, Dia. Forties, at the latest. I haven't danced in almost twenty years *and* I'm forty-one. It's not feasible."

Something drops inside me. "I ruined your career." I've known that for a long time, but I don't think I've said it out loud before.

Mom drops the pair of shoes in her hand back in their box, and sits beside me on a large velvet settee. "Listen to me, Nadia. I was born poor. Dirt poor, and in a bad neighborhood. Most days, I went to bed hungry. There was a rich old lady who felt bad for kids like me, so she opened a dance school. It was a charity, only a few hours a week. One day, she took me aside and told me I was good—really good. That if I worked hard, it could be my ticket out of there. I was eight, and hungry. In more than the physical sense. I needed more than what I had, you hear me?"

I nod, stunned and wondering how I didn't know any of that about my mother.

"Turned out, the lady used to be a professional dancer in her younger days. When my toes bled, I bandaged them and went back to my pointes. When I was twelve, she got some of her fancy friends to come see me. I got a scholarship and sponsorship to come here, to New York. I worked harder. I was still *hungry*. And when the money started rolling in, I killed myself on my toes to earn more." Silence falls and Mom shakes her head. "I needed dancing to survive, but now? I hate ballet, darling."

I blink, completely astonished. "But you teach ballet. You do classes..."

"At the youth club," she completes, looking at me expectantly.

Finally, the wheels turn and I understand. "You do it to help. Like the old lady helped you."

She smiles at me like she's proud. "Mind you, I'm nothing like that old crone. Mireille was a slave driver. She enjoyed the torture, I swear."

I recognize the name. "Auntie Mireille? You call her every year, right?"

Mom smiles, squeezing my shoulders. "I don't speak about my past often because it wasn't pretty, Dia. But without Auntie Mireille, I wouldn't be here."

I don't think she means in New York.

"So, no ballet. But don't you get, like, bored?"

Mom laughs out loud. "Hardly. I put money away when I was working, and invested it well. I get to have fun with my friends when I want to, and I can enjoy my own company, too. My life's very fulfilling, Dia, don't you worry about me." She kisses my forehead. "It's my job."

I notice she hasn't mentioned my father.

"How about you? When you've sold millions of wonderful art pieces and your name is on everyone's lips, what do you want? To find a job to avoid boredom?"

I wrinkle my nose, finding it hard to see that far down the road. "I don't know. One dream at a time, Mom."

She tilts her head. "Think about it, okay? As young people, we spend a lot of time working, and sometimes we miss the bigger picture."

That's unusually wise.

Before I can wallow in despair about finding the meaning of life, Mom squeals. "Oh my god! You *have* to try those shoes!"

Before I see them, I know she's wrong. Our tastes couldn't be more different. I like heavy, mostly flat, edgy boots I can customize. Mom likes four-figure stilettos.

She runs and comes back with a pair of shiny red shoes. I'm stunned because she's right. I have to try them on.

With a white rim and delicate yellow patent along the edge, the pumps have white heels with floral decorations. They're incredibly cute, and different. My mother wouldn't be caught dead in them, but they're definitely *me*.

"I don't normally wear heels."

"They're blocks, they won't hurt. You can always keep a pair of flats in your purse. Go on, try them."

I do, because those shoes are adorable.

My mother bounces up and down and herds me to a mirror. My eyes widen. I'm just wearing jeans and a plain purple sweater tied at the waist. My hair's in its usual messy bun. But somehow, with those shoes, I look different. Put together, as though I have an actual style.

"You need these shoes."

I bite my lip. I don't usually have a Saks budget.

"How much are they?"

"Tut-tut." Mom shakes her head. "You don't need to know. Go on. Wait for me downstairs—get us a table at L'avenue, yes? I'll take care of it."

I narrow my eyes. "Is that a Dolce & Gabbana logo?"

"Go!"

I do as I'm told.

They're very pretty shoes.

# CHAPTER TWENTY-FIVE

I don't look like me. I don't even feel like me. I stand taller, more intimidating, as if daring the world to come at me. Who knew all it took was an overpriced piece of footwear?

The pumps subtly echo the colors of the uniform, as if they were made just for me. My mom told me this specific style is called Mary Jane. What shoes have in common with Spiderman's love interest, I'll never know, but I love them all the same. I hadn't noticed when I tried them on, but their red exactly matches the trim of the Cross blazer. Our skirt is a checkered black and red, and there are thin blue and yellow lines mixed in it. Mom bought me a navy blue wool beret to complete the look when I wasn't paying attention.

These heels are magic. I even brushed my hair this morning, which is akin to a miracle. I tend to only bother after showering at night. Knowing it'll bother me if I let it hang loose around my eyes, I braid the front around my head, leaving the back alone.

I like the girl staring back at me in the mirror. She doesn't even look like a real student—she seems airbrushed, camera ready. The girl doesn't look much like Nadia Reyes, but maybe I'd like a break from being me. I apply some apple lip balm and smile at my reflection, wondering when the last time I did that was. Some night last summer when I was hanging out with my friends in New York, probably.

I remove the beret before exiting my room. It's a little too much for my taste. Besides, it doesn't go very well with my headphones, and those are an essential item for survival.

I wasted too much time this morning to sit down for breakfast. I just grab an apple and a cereal bar, discreetly eating both at the back of the bus before getting off in front of the courtyard.

"Jesus, Nadia!" Sophia's jaw hangs open. She does a full sweep from my feet to my hair, and blinks. I see her mouth tighten. She doesn't seem to like what she sees.

Too bad for her. I do.

"What happened!"

I snort. To hear her talk, my changing my shoes and hair might as well be a disaster. "I woke up early." Ish.

"That's *so* not your style."

Now she's getting on my nerves. "Well, tight shirts weren't yours last year."

The last bell rings through the school, announcing the start of the class. I take the cue to end this stupid conversation and take my seat. Part of me wants to distance myself from Sophia, but I'd rather avoid the drama so I take my usual place. We don't exchange a word in class. I'm only half paying attention, fuming and hurt at her attitude. Why is she making a big deal out of a good hair day and a nice pair of shoes?

I know the answer, but it doesn't make me feel better. She's insecure. Always has been. She's made changes that soothed her frayed self-esteem this year, and I suppose comparing her new look to my usual "I don't give a shit" appearance made her feel better. Seeing me try a little pisses her off.

Fuck her. That's not how real friends think. Come to think of it, we haven't been real friends at all this year. It drives home that we were just using each other in our solitude.

It would be a sin to drag these pretty heels, but I take my time making my way to literature after Italian, gliding in right as the class starts. I keep my headphones on, blasting Ed Sheeran loud enough to burst my eardrums. I rush to my seat, eyes stubbornly fixed on it, refusing to acknowledge Jason seated in the next row.

But I see him. Of course I see him. I even catch Cain smirk, punch Jason's arm, and tilt his head toward me before leaning back in his chair.

Jason doesn't pay his friend any attention, his gray eyes fixed on me. He's not smirking. His entire face has adopted a cold mask that should make me shiver. Everything's ice, except his gray eyes.

Part of me can't help remembering his arms around me. I tell that part to shut the hell up and remember literally everything else instead.

I sit, remove my headphones, and pull out my notebook.

"Thanks for joining us, Ms. Reyes. Now please remind us where we left off on Friday."

We're almost done with that play, thank god. I hadn't expected our class to go so in depth about *Romeo and Juliet*, but we're barely doing a scene a day. "Romeo had just killed Tybalt, sir."

"Just so. Now, we're rapidly approaching the end. Before we get there, I'd like you all to discuss the play today. I want you to pick one character you relate to and analyze their motivation, their hopes and fears. Everyone gets three minutes, and yes, you will be graded on your performance. You have ten minutes to get ready. I encourage discussion between you—ask your friends pertinent questions to ensure their presentation covers as much as possible."

On that note, Mr. Green leaves the room, abandoning us.

Melina laughs, turning to face me. "Bet you anything he has a hangover and didn't feel like teaching an actual class."

I'm too stunned she's speaking to me to form an immediate answer.

"*Love* the shoes. And it's clever, getting them a

year later, so no one else can get their hands on them."

I glance at my feet and shrug. "My mom bought them for me. I think there was a sale at Saks."

Melina nods sagely. "They tend to bring out old stock when they have big sales. I dig. And you're going to have to tell me how you do that braid."

I run my hand over the French braid crowning half my head. "It looks like a style, but it's mostly loose because I'm not very good at braiding."

"Stop with the humble nonsense, it makes me want to vomit. Cute shoes? On sale. Nice hair? Oh, I suck at braiding." She rolls her eyes. "Take a compliment, Reyes."

I smile at her, a little sadly because, well, that was what Sophia should have said in Italian class. What any friend ought to say, even if it wasn't true.

Melina twists in her seat, glaring behind me. "And don't get on my case about talking to her. Girl's fire today. Someone ought to tell her."

I don't turn, but I hear Cain chuckle. "The lady has a point."

"'Did anyone hear me say anything?" Jason wonders out loud.

Taking that as permission to keep chatting with me, Melina asks, "Right, who's the easiest character. Juliet, right? She's such a wet blanket."

I wrinkle my nose. "No way, there are too many layers to unpack. The treatment of women, Juliet's relationship with her mother, father, nurse, then also Paris and the Friar... If you want easy, go for

Benvolio or Mercutio. Benvolio's one dimensional, which could be its own issue—not much to say about him. Mercutio, though...he's interesting enough."

"Mercutio it is," Melina announces cheerfully, running through her notes. She glanced back at me, "Unless you wanted him, too?"

"Oh, no, pass. He's all yours."

"Something against Mercutio?" Jason asks.

My spine stiffens because he's speaking to me. Long seconds stretch in silence. I can feel the heat of his stare.

"Don't forget what happens when you ignore me," he remarks casually.

I do my best not to flinch and force a smile. "No," I reply, my tone flat. "Nothing against Mercutio."

Jason sighs. "'Thy wit is a very bitter sweeting; it is a most sharp sauce.'"

"How many quotes have you memorized?" I can't help asking.

"I have a good memory," he replies.

Cain snorts. "Yeah, right. Like that's cutting it. This guy? He never forgets a thing. Ever."

That must come in handy for school. No wonder he always ends up toward the top of the class. I'd wondered if it had been his daddy's money buying his grades. And it could still be.

"Not always," Jason corrects. "I forgot Nadia for a while."

Now I turn back to him, eyes widening.

He can't mean...

No, he can't possibly remember me from back then. He must mean he forgot my existence in the last three weeks, hence why he didn't bother harassing me directly. And to think I was stressing out every time I walked into this class, expecting him to do...I don't know what, exactly.

"So, who do you relate to, Nadia? Not loyal Mercutio or boring, loving Benvolio. Who?"

His full attention is on me, tuning out the rest of the class, as though my answer could be life and death.

"I guess you'll find out."

We're called by alphabetical order, so Jason's first. He picks Mercutio. That makes me chuckle under my breath. I know he doesn't relate to him even the tiniest bit. If Jason has to be cast as one character in that play, he's the Prince, dictating everyone's fate with a few imperious words.

He presents every argument with a deep understanding of both the play and the character, throwing in a few more quotes for good measure. His straight A in this class is well earned, to my frustration.

Melina's presentation is much weaker, but she pulls it off. Cain chooses Benvolio, and somehow manages to make the guy sound interesting. He's also a liar. He's Tybalt, as loyal as Mercutio, but indifferent to the fate of Verona. Right and wrong mean nothing to the Tybalts of the world. What matters is winning.

When it's my turn, I'm not the first to choose Romeo, but I'm the first to present my theory. "He's frustrated, bored, and depressed from the start and hides it from himself by flying from one crush to the next. If he hadn't died in three days, he would have found another love interest and cheated on Juliet at the first opportunity. I think Romeo's a modern teen, and therefore the character I can relate to most in the play. Unfulfilled, finding the rules of the adults in charge unjust and stifling."

Mr. Green nods. "Very good, Nadia. I wish we had more time to let you expound on that thread. For now, A plus. Next..."

# CHAPTER TWENTY-SIX

Out of habit, my stuff's packed by the time the bell rings after lit. I like to be ready to hightail it out of this class. Not that I'm capable of hightailing it anywhere today.

Mom lied. Those pretty, pretty shoes hurt just as much as I assumed they would. Admittedly, they may not hurt *her,* given the fact that she probably doesn't have any nerves left in her feet. The pain isn't crippling—I can walk, but I'm slower than usual. I'm using muscles I didn't even know existed in my shins and under my feet. I should have listened to Mom's advice and packed some flats. For the first time this year, I'm looking forward to PE, so I can change into gym shoes for a while.

"Romeo, hm?"

I sigh as Jason slides to my side like he belongs there. Cain joins us, flanking me to my left. To look at us, inches apart, you'd think we were the best friends in the world, which tells you all there is to know about appearances.

"I call bullshit. You're not flighty, depressed, and whatever else you said."

Now that makes me snort. "Fascinating how you think you know anything about me, Alden."

"Jace," he corrects smoothly. "And I do. I know you went for the clever, out-of-the-box answer in order to get an A."

Damn him for being right. "Like you were any more honest. Besides, I'm being bullied by megalomaniac asshole kids with mommy issues. Of course I'm depressed."

I'm not, strangely. Am I sad about losing Sophia's friendship? A little, at times, but fragile relationships of that kind aren't worth cultivating—or crying over. I was never popular in this school. This drama since the start of the year might sap my energy, but most days it doesn't truly hurt me.

Except last Friday. That art class bitch better stay the fuck away from me from now on. I have access to plenty of pointy objects in that class. If she "accidentally" messes with my stuff again, I'll "accidentally" stab her dominant hand.

Maybe not. I don't want to get expelled. And potentially arrested.

Jason's hand moves to my chin, holding it tight. He stops walking and tilts my head up so I meet his eyes. "Don't lie to me. Are you?"

I slap his hand away, hating the jolt of current I feel when he touches me. "What?"

"Depressed," he clarifies. "You don't seem to be."

My lips purse. "You don't know me, asshole. Don't act like you do. And don't act like you care. It makes me sick."

On that note, I rush on my way to the cafeteria, ignoring the pain in my feet.

Except, I'm still wearing heels, and his legs are ridiculously longer than mine, so he catches up without effort. If anything, we're probably walking at his normal pace now.

"Are you coming to the Halloween party?" Jason asks, like it's a natural question.

I remember him inviting me last week.

"Right. Why wouldn't I walk into the ostentatious dorm of the asshole who delights in tormenting me with all his friends?"

"Errr, because our parties are fucking epic, cupcake," Cain puts in. "DJs, booze, freshly baked pizza, cake, you name it. Hell, if you have a food or drink request, let us know—the school's still organizing."

I wrinkle my nose. "The school is providing booze for an underage party?"

Cain laughs. "Technically, Glass's a private residence. And, see, the booze is for our supervisors. We wouldn't *dream* of touching it. At least, not if you ask the faculty."

Unbelievable. I'm too astounded by the level of privilege these guys benefit from. Rules, *laws*? None of that matters in their world. They bend them to their will.

"Come on. It'll be fun," Cain promises, shooting me his megawatt smile.

"I've seen a dozen teen movies. This scenario doesn't end well for me. Or for you, if whatever you're planning involves pig's blood."

"Why would there be a plan?" Jason puts in.

My answer is immediate. "Because I'm not sure you take a shit without planning it."

Cain laughs like he's never heard a better joke, though I'm entirely serious. "She's got you there, man."

Jason's rare smile makes me uncomfortable. I hate how gorgeous he looks. It's unfair that such a terrible, selfish egomaniac can look like *that.* "How about a deal? Come, and your exile ends. I'll tell the school you've learned your lesson about sticking your nose where it doesn't belong. Everyone will back off."

Anger rises in my chest. "Fuck all the way off, Alden. The only lesson I've learned is that men like you don't deserve the air you breathe."

I turn on my heel, walking away from the cafeteria. I'm suddenly not hungry anymore. And I'd rather cut off a leg than spend another minute with that asshole.

He treats the world like we're inconsequential pawns, rising and falling at his pleasure. He's right, I'm not depressed. But if I had been, it would have been entirely on his shoulders. Some teenagers harm themselves because of the kind of bullshit he put me through over the last month.

I head to the courtyard. It's raining, so no one else came outside. I commandeer a bench and try to regain my composure with slow, steadying breaths.

I remove my shoes, propping them on the bench, and lie down with my feet up on the armrest. I think I fall asleep despite the rain. One moment I'm alone, eyes closed, trying to calm down. The next, I sit up, startled, feeling Jason's presence before he closes in on me.

He's hovering above me, holding out a brown paper bag.

"Can't you just leave me alone?" I'm practically moaning.

"No." He sits on the bench, taking my legs and moving them on top of his lap. Then he hands me the bag. "You have to eat."

Now that I'm less pissed, I am fairly hungry, but I hate to take anything from him. Maybe I can just head back to the cafeteria. I should have enough time to grab a sandwich.

But whatever's in the bag, it smells *good.*

"It's tacos," he clarifies. "From some small place in town."

My stomach grumbles and I snatch the bag from him. Sure enough, I'm greeted by the familiar aroma of the delicious taco stand I haven't had a chance to go back to since my second week at Cross.

Riding the bus to the dorm takes ten minutes—if

you can catch it immediately—then another five to walk to the parking lot, and the drive into town takes another five. If you count parking and waiting in line, I don't have time to get out during my lunch hour.

"How the hell did you get these?" I muse.

"I sent my driver out."

Of course he did.

I dig in, both because I'm hungry and because the humongous ass owes me tacos, at the very least.

I moan around the food, savoring the flavor. I've eaten half of it before I come up for air long enough to tell Jason, "I still hate you."

"You don't hate me, Nadia. I see you looking at me like you want a bite." He's certain, not even smug or teasing. Matter-of-fact.

"Of your carotid artery," I snap back, ignoring that my entire face caught fire.

I hate that he sees my greatest shame: the fact that despite everything he's done to me, everything I know about him, part of me is still inexorably attracted to him. I blame hormones. They fucking suck.

"Did the shoes take their toll?" he asks, glancing at my bare feet. "You're not used to heels."

"You have no clue what I'm used to."

He's right, of course. Bastard.

"That's the hill you're gonna die on? I know plenty about you, Nadia. The background search I had done on you was comprehensive. I have every school report. You were cute when you won that spelling bee championship. The pigtails were adorable. Every picture where you showed up online —you like partying. You should come to my club. I'd love seeing that blue sequin dress in person."

My jaw drops. "You're stalking me?"

"It's standard practice to know who you let into your life." He shrugs. "And no, although I considered making my PI tail you. You're far too vulnerable for an heiress. Still, I suppose you're safe enough for now."

"I'm *not* in your life. And I'm most definitely not an heiress."

His cocks an eyebrow, pissing me off, because I've always wanted to be able to do that—lifting just one, like a movie star.

"You don't know?" Jason seems perplexed. "Your uncle is leaving half his fortune to you—the other half goes to Lucas, naturally."

*What the fuck?* I blink, completely taken aback. "You must be mistaken."

Jason smiles again. "Comprehensive background check, remember?"

He takes one of my feet in his hands, ignoring my yelp, and presses a thumb hard on the sole of my foot. I scream in agony, jerking my foot, but his hold is firm. Before I can kick him with my free leg, he rubs around the spot he just pressed, and I arch my back, both pain and pleasure flooding through my entire body.

What is this sorcery?

"My mother wears heels every day. She has my father and me well trained in foot rubs."

I'm about to say something rude about his mother issues, but his fingers are unknotting all my tension and all I can do is whimper. And eat my tacos.

When he's done with my foot, he tackles the other. And I let him.

"I don't get you." There, I said it. I don't understand anything about him.

Admitting it takes some swallowing of my pride, because it suggests one truth I would have preferred to keep to myself: I want to get him. I want to understand what makes him tick. I always have.

Naturally, now I'd use that knowledge to bring him to his knees and make him beg for mercy for everything he's done to me.

In the distance, I hear the bell signaling the end of our lunch break.

I grimace, moving my legs and putting my shoes back on.

"Thanks," I say because I'm polite. "You're still an asshole."

He's a good sport about it. "Anytime, doll."

We walk back to the school building together in silence.

I set off toward the gym, willing myself to not look back at him, though I feel his gaze on me.

What the hell just happened?

Part of me doesn't want to know.

# CHAPTER TWENTY-SEVEN

The more I think about it, the more I realize I should be far more irate about many things. For one, it's absolutely not okay for Jason fucking Alden to research everything about my life. Standard practice, my ass. It's downright stalker-y. But there's nothing I can do about it, so I decide not to waste too much of my energy sparing him another thought.

The next day, when Lucas waves at me in the corridor, I zero in on him. "Did you know I'm in your dad's will?" I say, without so much as a hello.

My cousin simply shrugs. "Sure. That's news to you?"

My mind is blown by his casual indifference. *What the fuck?* "Yeah. Lucius didn't tell me, nor did you, for that matter."

The first bell rings, but I fix my gaze on my cousin, unrelenting. He sighs. "Look, we can talk about it with Dad, but it's pretty simple. Dad has money, and he loves you." With a shrug, he adds, "Plus, you know how it is with company shares. Dad built the company—the investors trust him to have its best interest in mind. Me? I'm a wild card, regardless of how much time I spend working there. I could go crazy and devalue their stock. Splitting his fifty-one percent ensures I won't have too much power when I take over."

"I'm getting half of the company?" I practically yell.

*Oh, no. No, no, no.*

So, one thing about my uncle. I love him. He loves me. I trust him to have my best interest at heart in all things. But I decided long, long ago that I never wanted to get anywhere close to his business.

When he was young and his parents moved from Italy, his dad couldn't easily find a job with his broken English, so he reached out to a cousin who gave him some work. It was dodgy as fuck, although I don't know the details. All I know is that my uncle and his brother walked away from all that, never getting involved.

This is the pretty version, wrapped in a red bow and covered in unicorn sprinkles, that I am going to die believing. Because, as I said, I love my uncle. And I'm smart enough to stick to that.

I've seen him take meetings with the cousins he's officially not doing business with. I've heard some of his phone calls. I've seen blood on his collar. I know what he does isn't always clean, and I can read between the lines.

Astrella Public Relations does exactly what it says on the sign: it makes people—and companies—look good. And to make the assholes running the world appear like decent human beings? Well, it doesn't just take graphic designers, charity galas, and pictures with adorable babies.

Therefore, I've promptly ignored all the incriminating evidence I've ever heard, seen, or guessed. I trust Uncle Lucius to never do anything evil. He has a strong grasp of justice. He wouldn't crush an old lady to help a giant. That's all I need to know.

But I sure as fuck do not ever want to have *anything* to do with Astrella PR. Nuh-uh.

"Half of his shares," Lucas clarifies. "Like, after his death. Which isn't going to happen for a long, long time. What's the big deal?"

I could strangle my cousin, but it's not his fault. I need to have a chat with my uncle, and soon.

The last bell rings, so I shake my head. "See you later."

I run to calculus. As the teacher isn't here yet, I text my uncle. **Brunch Sunday?**

He immediately replies. **I'm out of town. Next Sunday?**

I send a thumb up and I try to shelve all of my questions until then.

The morning drags, until I realize with some

horror that I'm looking forward to literature. What the hell is wrong with me? I should go see a shrink.

I spot Cain at his usual place as soon as I walk in. Jason's seat is empty. I frown, unused to seeing Cain without him.

Cain catches my eye, and answers the question I'm too proud to ask. "He's in the city today. Some business with his father. But I'll let him know you care."

I bristle. "I didn't say anything."

"Right. I suppose you always stare at me with puppy dog eyes, then."

I shoot him the finger before taking my seat, telling myself I'm relieved. Too bad I'm such a terrible liar.

I grab a sandwich at the cafeteria and head out of doors, because for the first time in a while, it's actually sunny.

I'm not surprised to see a few students gathered in the courtyard—I don't get the place to myself unless the weather's terrible. As I approach the row of benches, I frown, realizing they're all converging around the first bench, where Jason gave me a foot rub yesterday.

It's an odd mix of students. Judith and Manon Montgomery don't typically hang out with gangly teens like Peter March and Albert Franklin.

"We should call someone," Albert says. "A teacher or something."

"Already done," Manon replies imperiously. The

ebony beauty actually acknowledged the geek's existence.

I can't help it. I get close and go up on tiptoe to get a view of what they're all looking at.

Then I scream.

# CHAPTER TWENTY-EIGHT

I march straight back into the school, heading to the cafeteria, bile and fury rising at every step.

When I get there, I stride straight to Their Majesties' table and plant my palms flat on it. "That's crossing a fucking line!" I don't care if I'm screaming. I don't care if I look crazy.

Cain and Maverick exchange a look, while Rowan stares at me, apparently entertained.

"I'll burn your fucking world for this, if it costs me everything. You make sure to pass the message along."

I've said my piece, and I walk away, rushing to get to the bathroom before I barf right there in front of everyone. The entire school is staring. I don't fucking care.

"Wow, cupcake." Cain catches up with me and grabs my wrist.

I turn and throw a punch. Unfortunately, he's as skilled as Jason at blocking them.

"You're going to have to expand on that little scene," he tells me. "We didn't do anything."

I spit in his face.

Cain grimaces and wipes it with the back of his letter jacket. "I'll allow that, because you look upset." As an afterthought, he adds, "And I probably deserve it. But, cup..."

I snatch my hand back and try to slap him.

"Sorry, sorry. *Nadia*. Something's wrong. Like, really wrong. Tell me what it is, and I'll help."

He sounds oh so sincere. For the shadow of a second, I question myself.

Then I tell him, "Go to hell," and walk away.

In the bathroom, I vomit the entire contents of my stomach. I should have vomited it on Cain and the rest of them. Frustration coils inside me, hating that the real culprit isn't here.

Jason did this.

Maybe not directly, but he's marked me as a target for whatever sick reason.

I sink down on the tile floor and cry.

When my eyes close, I see it. I recognized Cat on sight, even without its head.

What kind of sick person decapitates a fucking cat? A psycho, that's who.

Guilt and anger keep me glued to my cubicle past the bells, for I don't know how long. I don't even consider heading to PE.

I'm still sitting down, tearstained, numb, and cold, when footsteps sound outside.

"Come out."

I'm stunned, and not only because it's a male voice in the girls' bathroom.

"What are you doing here?" My voice sounds wrong to me. Hoarse. I suppose crying does that to you.

"Cain told me to get back here," Jason replies. "Come out, Nadia."

Not doll or cupcake today.

"Fuck you."

"Happy to oblige any other time," he shoots back. "Just not right now. Come on, Nadia, I need to see you."

Because he likes seeing me in pain.

I must have said it out loud because he replies, "I don't. Not even a little bit."

I snort. "Go away."

I hear a sigh, and then a commotion that makes the walls of the cubicle vibrate. Seconds later, Jason appears on top of the toilet, having somehow climbed the partition. He jumps on the closed toilet seat and joins me, getting on his knees so we're at the same level.

"You look terrible," he informs me.

"Better than being a terrible person." That's a weak comeback, but it's all I have.

He humors me with a chuckle, then brushes one of my curls away from my face.

"I heard about Bella."

I wrinkle my nose. "Who's Bella?"

"The cat," he explains. "She was Ms. Casey's."

Somehow, hearing that makes me feel worse.

Ms. Casey's the one member of the school faculty who's been kind to me—even helpful. Now her cat is dead because some asshole wants to fuck with me to please the guy who jumped in my toilet stall with me.

How crazy is that?

"It's your fault," I inform him.

He might not have been at school today, but he did it all the same when he chose to single me out and set the hounds on me.

He nods. "It is. I'd undo it if I could."

"Then leave me alone. Go bother someone else. The school will stop if you just stay away from me."

Jason shakes his head. I should have known. He won't give me that.

I can't deal with him. I get to my feet, unlock the stall, and walk out. Out of this school. I make my way to the dorm on foot, needing the air.

Jason follows me wordlessly. "My mother was stabbed once," he says, breaking the almost comfortable silence.

I glance at him, because I'm too surprised to do what I decided seconds ago: ignore him.

"In the street. Someone bumped into her, just stabbed her and ran away. It's a miracle she survived. All her friends smile at her, treat her like she's the most important person in their life, but it was one of them who hired the thug. We found the responsible party—with your uncle's help, actually."

What the hell?

"What happened to the one who hired the thug?"

"She's dead," he states casually.

My head is going to explode. "Why are you telling me this?"

Ignoring my question, Jason says, "Some scars are harder to heal. When I was eight, I was kidnapped." He shakes his head. "Well, we were—Alexander and I."

I freeze in horror. Oh, no. He's not going there. Not now. I can't take it today.

"Our kidnapper brought us to a cabin in the woods. As he was dragging us inside, I managed to run away and bring help back."

I'm shaking my head, sobs clogging my throat. "Jason..."

"By the time we got back, Alexander, my twin, was dead. He'd been murdered. I should have been, too."

I didn't know the details. I'd been too young to ask, and besides, I don't think the news talked about a murder at all.

"It was my uncle, Tristan," Jason said. "See, the Aldens might have had old money, but most of the family squandered, their trust fund, whereas my father built an empire. After starting his political career and leaving his company, he hired his brother as CEO. Tristan had smoked, drunk, gambled, and fucked away all of his money, but my father knew Tristan was smart enough for the job. They could use each other and be one happy family." Jason's jaw is shut tight. "Tristan lost it when my brother and I were born. Somewhere in his mind, he was my father's heir. The company belonged to him. We threatened that. So he decided to eliminate the threat."

I'm appalled.

"Your uncle worked that out, too," Jason said. "His team was already on the way to the woods with my dad by the time I escaped. They caught my uncle trying to flee. Do you know what happened then, Nadia?"

Of course I know. They killed the bastard who'd murdered an eight-year-old. I would have too.

"It's not just the occasional attack. There are rumors following my family all the time—hurtful things. We all grew thick skins to deal with it."

"That's not an excuse." I'm shaking my head. "None of this. Just because your life is crappy doesn't give you the right to make mine a nightmare, too."

"I'm not looking for any excuse," he replies. "You once asked me why I did this to you. I'm answering you. You've been part of my life for ten years, Nadia. A ghost I see when my eyes are closed. You could be part of my life for the next ten, twenty, fifty years. I needed to see you could take it. The madness that comes with being an Alden."

I stare at him in utter disbelief.

No.

Just no.

"You're joking." I can't imagine another reason.

"Do I ever joke?"

"Well, you are now. I don't believe you."

Jason shrugs. "I don't see why. I made my intentions clear from the start. I want you, Nadia. That's dangerous for you. And now we both know you can deal with danger. You fight your own battles. You don't run to the nearest authority figure expecting them to fix shit for you. And you keep a cool facade no matter how you feel inside."

"So, what, you were tormenting me to test me? That's sick. You're sick."

He nods. "Most definitely. And you still want me. Even after today."

My stomach drops as I see poor Bella's broken body again.

He reads my expression well enough to know what I'm thinking about. "I promise I never asked anyone to hurt the cat, Nadia. Or break your artwork, for that matter."

"You have zealous fans," I snarl bitterly.

"And zealous enemies," he replies, his mouth tightening. "I'll protect you from both if you let me. We can make a deal."

We're almost at the dorm. And a good thing too; I need time to think, to process everything he just said.

“What sort of a deal?”

He tilts his head, thoughtful. “I’ll think about it and get back to you.”

“I’m *not* dating you," I tell him. Just because *he* decided he wanted me doesn't give him the right to interfere in my life to this extent. I'm simply not letting him get away with it.

He snorts. "I didn't ask you out."

"Well, so long as we're in agreement." Then I ask, "What do you want from me? Seriously." I'm just confused by this point.

Jason smiles. "Everything. When you're ready for it."

"I still don't believe you," I say honestly. "When you locked me in my room and touched me, you did it because you loved seeing me helpless. I could tell. That wasn't a test. That was your kink."

He smirks. "And you liked it. I would have stopped if you didn't. I only came to give you a burger."

My mouth gapes. The nerve of this guy! I slap his arm, without much heat.

We've reached the doors of the dorm. He brings his lips to my forehead, dropping a light kiss there. "Go, rest up. Brush your teeth."

"Fuck you!"

"Definitely. After you brush your teeth."

I stay at the doors, dumbfounded, as I watch him walk away.

What was that all about?

# CHAPTER TWENTY-NINE

Somehow, I survive the weirdest week of senior year so far.

After our chat on Tuesday, Jason mostly ignores me. Well, that's not quite accurate. He says hi to me every morning. He occasionally asks how I'm doing. That's it. And more strangely yet, the rest of the school takes a cue from their leader and stops treating me like a leper.

I spend the entire week nervous on several levels. This feels like the calm before the storm. Jason has schemes, plans within plans. I don't doubt he's been honest with me. He's always direct, something I've grown to appreciate. He also didn't tell me everything. If he was truly interested in me, he would have insisted I date him. There's more. I don't think I want to find out how much more. Not yet.

I work at my dad's restaurant, Mio Cuore, that Friday night. I didn't ask for a shift, but I'm barely out of Hulk after driving home from Cross when he begs me to help him out. Apparently, the flu season started and half of his staff's out. After the pandemic issues of the last couple of years, whenever someone's coughing, he wants them out of the building. It's safer that way for his business, but that means he can be desperate for staff from time to time.

I'm always happy to make minimum wage plus tips, so I get dressed in my depressingly classical black dress and white apron, and head to work.

I'd like to say it went well. I'd like to say nothing weird happened. I'd also like to win the lottery, pretty please.

I'm almost off the clock at ten when a group is directed to my section.

Seeing my classmates behind their menus, I groan.

*Really?*

Two tables of eight were put together to accommodate a dozen legacies. Among them, I note my kind-of-friends Melina, Judith, and Manon, as well as Ms. Perfect Yuki and Jacqueline Billington, my least favorite among the Barbie squad. The rest of them are too classy to bully their way to the top of the school hierarchy like the Brooke Vaughns of the world, but Jack? She loves nothing more than to belittle anyone she deems inferior. She was a bitch to Sophia for years, and since September she's made a point of laughing at me, though she, like the rest of the legacies, keeps her hands clean. She isn't the kind of idiot who'd trip me or call me names in public. The legacies are puppetmasters, not sheep.

Cain, Rowan, Maverick, and naturally, Jason, also grace me with their presence, along with a few guys I can't stand—Christoph Billington, Martin Lee, and a couple of guys I can't name off the top of my head. The girls wouldn't be caught dead in a small, traditional Italian restaurant that's never been mentioned in any fashionable magazine if Their Majesties hadn't dragged them here.

I plaster my best smile on my face, swallowing any hint of humiliation at serving fellow students at my school.

"Hey, my name is Nadia, and I'll be your waitress today." I beam, wanting to stab myself. Or maybe just stab Jason. I'd be good with that.

Knowing he's doing this on purpose, to see how I react, infuriates me a lot more than when I had no clue what was going on.

Like, how dare he? Seriously. I call bullshit. He's decided he wants to figure out if I fit into his world, without even asking me whether I have any interest in being part of it.

*Newsflash, asshole: I don't. And also, you suck. And you smell.*

*Exquisite. You smell fucking exquisite.*

Which doesn't matter. No one cares about Jason Alden's custom cologne.

"Can I get you anything to drink?"

Jason's eyes cut to me and he smiles. "Hi, Nadia. I'll have a glass of wine, if you would."

I could roll my eyes. He's eighteen. Which would be just fine if we were in Italy, but we aren't, so, he can fuck all the way off. I'm not getting fined for serving a minor, thanks.

His pointed stare tells me he's basically guessing every single one of my thoughts right now. He's waiting for my reaction, weighing it, assessing it. I expect he's ready for a conflict. I have no doubt if I ask for an ID, he'd provide one with the right date of birth, stumping me.

I fucking hate him.

"Coming right up. Anything else, guys?"

I don't want to be predictable. And I'm sure he has several IDs in his pocket in case we get checked, so whatever.

The rest of the table orders wine, beer, and cocktails. Which is just fine so long as they tip me well.

"What's the special tonight, Nadia?" Jason asks me.

"Eggplant bruschetta as a starter and orecchiette with zucchini flowers, pork sausage, and smoked cheese as an entrée."

"Jesus!" Cain yells. "That sound downright illicit. Is that legal? I'll have all of that, pretty please."

Scribbling his order, I smile despite myself. The asshole can be charming when he wants to be.

"How can you work here and look like you do?" Judith asks me. "I'd get fat in no time."

I laugh. "I suppose I'm used to it. My dad's the chef. When he cooks at home, pasta's just a small course—we eat a healthier starter and main." That's a lot more honesty than I should give those guys. They use truth as ammunition. I clear my throat. "I recommend the spaghetti frutti di mare," I say, because shellfish is the most expensive option.

My favorite is the good old carbonara, but they don't need to know that.

I jot down all their orders, glad to see each of them goes for a starter and an entrée.

Jason's last. "I'll have the spaghetti carbonara, *per favore*, Nadia." He slips into Italian with ease, like it's a comfortable shoe.

My eyes narrow on him. "*Sei sicurò? Il pesce alla griglia è squisito.*"

"*Ho gusti semplici, cara.*"

His accent's better than mine, though I hear a few errors. I sigh, huff, and turn on my heels to give the orders to the kitchen.

He's not in the Italian class, that I know of. What was that about?

I ask the bartender to prepare their drink order and run them two platters of complimentary antipasti. I'm tense as heck when I bring them to the table, not sure what to expect from them. Some bullying or mockery, no doubt.

Judith smiles brightly at me. "It looks amazing, Nadia, thanks!"

"For real. Italian food is just so Americanized in most restaurants," Melina says. "I haven't seen such a good platter since Rome last year."

I manage a smile, still waiting for the other shoe

to drop. "Thanks. Every ingredient comes directly from Italy, or is locally sourced." I give them the usual pitch, pointing to the various cured meats on their platters and letting them know where they're from.

Rowan rushes to try everything as I name them, and comments with appreciative moans and thumbs-up. I finally chuckle. "Don't choke on that, stupid."

He grins with his mouth full. Gross. "It'd be worth dying for."

Andrea, the bartender, catches my eye to let me know he's done with the drinks.

I go to collect them, serve them, and check on my other tables, always conscious of the group. They act like normal young people out on Friday night, barely sparing me a look. Part of me relaxes. The other part of me wonders what the fuck is going on. Jason tells me he wants me to be part of his life, then he leaves me alone for a week, and now he's coming to my dad's restaurant and...leaving me alone? If that guy's still playing a game, screwing with my head this time, I don't like it one bit, and it makes me want to screw with his right back.

We approach the end of my shift as they finish their starters. Normally, I notify all my tables that I'll be going, but this time, I slip out without a word, letting Jenny deal with the fallout. I'm sure Jason had a plan. He wanted to corner me, or say something to get under my skin. I don't let him.

# CHAPTER THIRTY

Our townhouse is close to the restaurant. I walk back in less than ten minutes.

Jason would be surprised if he saw our house. It's nice. Dad bought it the year Mom got pregnant. Nineteen years ago, Brooklyn was less trendy, and much cheaper. Nowadays, it would cost a pretty penny. There's nothing luxurious inside; it's cozy and comfortable, with a beige leather sofa and warm wood accents.

Mom always calls the house Dad's house. I see why. It's nothing like her. Her room and mine are the only touches of color. Hers, royal blue, with tons of velvet and silk. My walls are painted grayish purple, with silvery wallpaper on one wall. The princess bed I chose at twelve is ridiculous, but also humongous and ultra comfortable.

In my bedroom, I strip out of my work clothes and run to shower.

Jason's background check was right: I totally do

like to party. Not every week, and usually not during the school year, but I tend to dance with my city friends as soon as I have half an excuse to do so. We haven't met up in a while, but this is Halloween weekend. The thirty-first falls on a Monday this year, so we decided to celebrate it tonight.

A couple of my girls, Tara and Olivia, work at my dad's restaurant. They're both over twenty-one, so they tend to order drinks for us. Harper, Evie, Gabriella, and Spencer attend my old school.

I get changed into a short green dress frayed at the hems, ripped tights, my favorite comfortable boots, and work on my over-the-top makeup to complete the look of a dark witch. I'm placing my pointy hat on my wavy, messy hair when Mom knocks at my door. I know it's her because Dad will be at work until at least one in the morning.

"Yes?"

She's already walking inside. "Damn!" she screams, bringing her hands to her gaping mouth. "When did you grow so big?"

"Mom, that's downright embarrassing."

She rifles through the designer bag at her side, pulling out a string of foil packets. "Take those with you. I'm too young to be a grandma."

*Someone shoot me, please.* "In the near future, I'm going to waste all my money on a psychologist to get over this very moment."

She folds the six rubbers and hands them to me. "But you won't be doing it with a baby in tow. You're welcome."

I want to tell her I don't intend to use any of them, but to be fair, I lost my virginity on a night not unlike tonight last year. I hadn't intended to do anything but dance and drink a little back then, either. I take the condoms and fit them into my pouch as she moves to my dressing table and fusses with my makeup bags.

She brings a brush to my face. I close my eyes and let her play doll. By the time she's done, my makeup's changed, going from dramatic to slightly more natural, and ten times more striking. I don't know how she does it.

"Thank you, Mom." I notice she looks particularly pretty, even by her standards.

Her clothes are the opposite of mine. She's in an off-white jumpsuit with a deep neckline, and a heavy gold chain studded with diamonds hangs on her chest. She pairs it with gold heels and a luxurious fur coat—I know it's fake because she'd never wear real fur, but it doesn't look it.

"Doing something special tonight?" I ask her.

She shrugs. "Nothing exciting. And you, who are you going out with?"

"The usual group. Everyone's coming. It's been a while."

Given my work shift, I'll be the last one to arrive, so I have to double-check where they are before heading out. I pull out my phone and check my messages, intending to open the group chat with my NYC friends. Instead, I notice a message sent from an unknown number.

**Running away? That's not like you, doll.**

My hand tightens on my phone.

"Anyone I know?" Mom asks with a wicked grin, shamelessly spying.

I pocket my phone, about to say no. Then I remember. Mom knows Jason. Well, that might be an exaggeration, but she's met him at least once, at his brother's funeral.

"A guy from my school," I hedge.

My mother beams. She's like a cat who got the cream. "Any guy who makes you blush like that, I should know about." She sits on my bed and pats the mattress next to her. "Tell me."

I bite my lip. *Well, Mom, he got the entire school to bully me to see if I had thick skin, then when he established I did, he started to ignore me.* Yeah, right. There's nothing I could talk to my mother about regarding Jason fucking Alden. If I told her half of what he's been up to, she'd have his balls.

"Nothing much to tell. He's a legacy." She knows the term—I've mentioned it a few times.

Mom lifts an eyebrow. "Oh." Her voice's an octave higher than normal. Then she clears her throat. "I, mm. I see."

I tilt my head, curious now. There's definitely a *tone* to those few words. "Mom?"

She's looking at everything except me. "Well, I'd better get going. You can tell me all about the boy tomorrow, yes?"

Oh, boy. I'm *not* letting that go.

"Mom, what do you know?"

She's trying to leave. Ah! I use her method for whenever I try to run away from a particularly embarrassing situation, and tackle her from behind, wrapping my arms around her. "Mom, spill. Whatever makes you look that way, I need to know."

She sighs and turns around, wincing. "I'm not the best person to talk about that kind of thing to you, Dia, sweet. I'm your *mother*."

I have no idea what she's talking about, but everything in me tells me I need to push this.

"Do you know any legacies?" I counter.

She sighs. "No. Of course not. The legacies are children." She wrinkles her nose in distaste. "Well, young people, like you. You know what I mean."

I don't. I'm completely lost.

"The legacies," she says after a long pause, "are the children of the members of the Heritage private club, Dia."

I knew that. The Heritage is a huge club right off Fifth Avenue. Their building dominates almost a whole block. They organize galas, charities, those sorts of things.

"So?"

Mom purses her lips, weighing her words more carefully than she usually does. "They lead a different life. I..." She shakes her head. "I don't know how to tell you, and it doesn't matter much anyway, unless the boy's serious about you. Is he?" Her eyes widen. "You've never talked about him before. Is...are you involved? Do you love him, Dia?"

I choke on a laugh, almost chuckling. Then I shake my head wordlessly, astonished she'd even ask. Of course I don't love Jason. Not even a little bit. I'm attracted to him, because, well, I have eyes. And I find him magnetic, fascinating, intriguing. I see a pleasing surface and all I want to do is dig deeper, scratch his skin away until I get to his soul.

I'm captivated. That has nothing to do with... that other word.

"Ah." Mom tries to smile. "Well, I'm not going to get into it, okay? But if you want to make room for this boy in your life, I want you to have an open mind, all the while paying attention to what you want—what you feel. Can you do that?"

I stare at my mother, a thousand questions flying around my brain.

I hear her, though. She's not the one I should get answers from.

"I can do that."

# CHAPTER THIRTY-ONE

My phone's burning in my purse, demanding my attention. I resist the temptation of pulling it out for a whole hour.

It's on silent, but I felt it vibrate twice, and I know who's texting me.

"How's your uppity school going? Turned you into a mini–Stepford Wife yet?" Harper asks me.

I roll my eyes. "I don't know, did yours turn you into a bitch yet?"

I'm kidding. Harper has always been a bitch. But she's *my* bitch.

We attended school together from first grade until I transferred to Cross. While we don't have time to hang out during the school year, especially back when I stayed on campus on weekends, we've caught up every chance we get. I suppose being in a school full of rich, privileged kids who don't stop to give me the time of the day made me cling to my old crew.

Harper lives a few blocks down from me, on the same street as Spencer. They date on and off, breaking up when Spencer feels like dating Trevor from the soccer team instead. Harper doesn't seem to mind.

Evie joined up when we were ten, having moved from California. She's your typical bleach blonde, athletic LA girl, except she has a soul. I think. She came with her mom after a messy divorce.

Gabriella was more Evie's friend than ours, originally. They met up on the cheerleading squad. She's cold and doesn't have tons of time for us, but she did stab Ben Williams with a fork when the guy copped a feel of Evie's breast without asking, so I pestered her to hang out with us until we became close friends. She'd totally stab some guy for me now. Maybe I should introduce her to Jason.

Or not. Gabriella's hot.

Too late, I recognize that this line of thought sounds far too close to jealous. *Like, what the fuck, Nadia? Seriously.*

Tara and Olivia took me under their wing when I started to work at my dad's restaurant when I was sixteen. They might be three or four years older than the rest of us, but we started hanging out together by default, because I finished working at the same time as them and they never wanted me to walk to my friends' by myself.

We have a full table, between our group and a

couple of guys who try to include themselves, hoping to score. One of them is cute, with his dark hair and full mouth, but I'm not even remotely interested. I think he said his name was Paul. When he bends his head to ask me if I want to dance, coming too close to my ear, I smile and point to my ear to pretend I can't hear him. I could tell him to fuck off, but at first, I generally try for a soft rejection if I can. When guys won't take the hint, I change tactics.

He comes even closer and yells, "Wanna dance!" His eyes peer down the top of my dress.

*Seriously, dude?* I don't even have that much cleavage. I'd totally understand if a guy couldn't help looking down Gabriella's shirt, but mine?

"No, thanks!"

I want to dance, just not with him.

To cut the conversation short, I pull out my phone, realizing too late that I'm not supposed to touch the device.

Now it's burning in my hand, begging me to check my messages.

*Dammit.*

I open the app, bringing my cosmo to my lips.

**Ignoring me? Oh, Nadia, you know that never ends well.**

Then right after, Jason sent, **Come to my club. You're owed a fair few consequences.**

He attached a dark picture. Opening it, I see a barcode in white, followed by a logo that read ME in an elaborate script.

"Holy fuck!" Paul, or whatever his name is, yells in my ear. "Is that real?"

He's staring at my phone, and I decide I need to sit somewhere else.

"Excuse me."

He doesn't seem inclined to. "You have a Midnight Elite invite? What are we doing here then?"

I have no clue what he's talking about.

"I need to go to the restroom. Have a nice evening."

I catch Gabriella's eye. She's a cute preppy girl, with long lashes over pale gray eyes and dark blonde hair. People generally underestimate everything about her.

More fool they.

I start to move away, and Paul-the-Idiot grabs my wrist, holding me in place.

Gabriella moves faster than anyone else. She snatches her empty cocktail glass and slams it against his face. Luckily for the asshole, the glass doesn't break, but he screams all the same, falling back down on the bench.

My group gets up, even those who hadn't noticed the situation, all rising to hide Paul from any bouncer who might have been looking our way.

"What the fuck?" Paul's friend, who'd been making out with Evie, says, wide-eyed.

Evie snarls at him. "You and your asshole friend can go. You don't mess with my girls."

She doesn't even know what happened, but the bottom line is, it doesn't matter.

Paul looks like he wants to charge at Gabriella.

Spence is pretty chill, but at six foot one, when he puffs his chest up and glares, most guys take notice and back off. He places himself in front of Gabriella, protective.

I missed this. I wish I had all of them with me at Cross.

Come to think of it, I think I dealt with the bullshit this year because I knew whatever happened in the school didn't matter. Here in the real world, I have people who have my back.

Reading the room, Paul's friend pats his shoulder and drags him out of our booth. "Come on, they aren't worth it. There's better pussy out here."

"I'm your first choice and you know it, asshole," Evie says with a wink.

A bruise is starting to form on Paul's brow—even in the dim light, it's hard to miss. I laugh as he passes in front of me, glaring but knowing he's in for more than he can chew if he tries anything with us.

They're shuffling away toward the dance floor when Gabriella turns her attention back to me. "Now, what was the idiot saying about you having a Midnight Elite invite?"

## CHAPTER THIRTY-TWO

Midnight Elite is a club. No, it's *the* club.

I haven't heard about it yet, but it opened last year and immediately became the place to be for anyone under thirty in the city. All the magazines mentioned it, there were paparazzi at the entrance because celebrities came in all the time. But the club had a strict guest list, and only let in a few people picked out of the crowd amassed in front every night.

The invite on my phone is apparently rarer than Willy Wonka's Golden Ticket.

Of course New Yorkers were fascinated: they love nothing more than a highly exclusive, inaccessible venue.

I google the club, a sneaking suspicion in mind. Bullseye. *"Midnight Elite was founded by four talented young men: J. Alden, C. Warren, M. Eaton, and R. White, who turned an old, failing bar into a huge success seemingly overnight."*

The article I'm reading doesn't mention the fact that they're all sons of megazillionaires who were given a stack of money to play with.

That's the club that started all my problems. The club where Judith was getting high. I should stay the fuck away from it, if only because Jason invited me.

Only a few problems. I'm tipsy, and I like to party. Most of all, I'm *really* curious.

I shoot Jason an answer. **Who's this?**

His response is almost immediate. An eye-roll emoji.

**My mama told me not to talk to stalkers.**

**Your mama would approve of me. Promise. Come on. I don't bite. Much.**

My fingers hover over the phone.

Yesterday, I would have thought his reply was just a jest, but after the awkward, strange conversation with Mom, I ask, **You know my mom?**

Jason takes a few minutes this time.

**I know of your mom.**

I'm biting my lower lip, wondering what he means.

**Come to me and I'll tell you how.**

Dammit. He knows me too well. I hesitate.

**I'm with friends. I'm not ditching them.**

**How many?**

**Six.**

**Done. Your invitation will cover all of you.**

Something holds me back still. Maybe the fact that it feels like a trap.

I look around at six expectant faces, staring at me while I was focusing on my phone like an asshole.

"You guys want to go to Midnight Elite?" I ask weakly.

No one says no, so we pay our bill and head out into the cold.

---

The club is in Hell's Kitchen, so we stack into two taxis, on account of Harper and Olivia's heels. My boots are mostly flat, so I could have walked, but it's cold, and I'm not wearing my warmest coat; I went for cute over practical, picking a red leather jacket.

When the taxi stops in front of thc club, I immediately feel silly and underdressed. There's a crowd amassed in front of two closed doors, with dozens of gorgeous model-worthy girls in short, sexy dresses, airbrushed to perfection. The guys are no less sophisticated. Their hair and clothes make them look like they're starring in a TV show. And I'm wearing ripped tights and a witch's hat.

My friends weren't kidding: there are paparazzi lining up—not in front of the crowd, but at another door, also blocked by a bouncer, but wide open. There's no line at all. I notice a bar code above the door.

I gesture my friends to the open door, as they'd started to make their way toward the crowd. *Here goes nothing.*

"Hey." I smile weakly at the bouncer, who looks like he chews metal bars for breakfast and spits out thumbtacks. "I have an invite."

He says nothing as I pull out my phone and show it to him.

His glower clears, and he grabs a device from his back pocket, scanning the barcode.

Then, to my utter horror, the herculean guard smiles. He looks pretty hot when he does. Which is disturbing, as he's rather terrifying.

There's something wrong with me.

"Ms. Reyes. A pleasure." He takes a step back to let us in.

The entrance is a mindfuck.

Pitch black, other than dim diamond lights dotting the floor, it makes me feel disoriented as fuck, although I just came out of another club.

I walk slowly, hanging on to a hand—Harper's, I think.

I don't know how far we've walked in terrified silence when a deep voice booms, "Welcome to the Elite."

Automatic doors swing open in front of us, and I enter another world.

There are women swaying on a hoop impossibly high on the ceiling. They're wearing almost nothing that I can see—maybe just diamond stickers. Although, it could be a cleverly designed costume—

I can't tell from here. A couple of women dance up and down aerial silks, sensual and dangerous.

The music blasting is a deep beat I immediately want to dance to. Most of the crowd is in agreement: they're dancing on the floor. I notice the DJ at the back—and my jaw drops.

"Is that Markus!" Spencer screeches.

I can only nod in wonder. He's the most famous DJ in the city. I attended one of his raves about two years ago, and I'm pretty sure that's *why* I love partying, and dancing. His music makes me feel free.

The servers are recognizable by the fact that they hold silver trays, and that they're various degrees of naked.

They're closer than the athletes on the ceiling, so I can tell they *are* wearing clothes. Just not much of it. All employees, male and female, are in flesh-colored mesh with cleverly placed patches of silver, for the Caucasian servers, or gold, for the darker-skinned people.

It's on the border between hot and vulgar, tilting more towards the latter.

The booths against the walls are made of soft leather with metallic studs and polished steel coffee tables, but only a few are occupied—almost everyone's dancing.

The bar occupies the center of the cavernous room, and right behind it I see a grand staircase designed like it belongs in an opera, but made of brushed silver. It leads up to a second floor, though

I wouldn't have guessed there was one, the ceiling is so high.

My friends hurry to the bar and I follow, gawking as I look everywhere.

I recognize faces. Not from school, but from billboards, fashion magazines, and TV shows.

*Holy fuck!*

"You like?"

I turn to face Yuki, blinking in surprise. I don't think I've ever spoken to her before, other than to ask her about her food order earlier today.

"Hell yeah." I scream back to be heard over the beat.

She's smiling at me, though it doesn't reach her eyes.

"I helped design this place," she tells me. "It's a resounding success, like everything Jason does."

I hold her stare. "I thought the four of them created it."

She rolls her eyes. "They bankrolled it and occasionally had some input, but this place? It's Jason's. Can't you feel it?"

I don't know what to answer. I don't know Jason enough to form an opinion, which I suppose is her point.

"You guys used to date," I mention.

Yuki seemed delighted by my comment. "You know. As much as Jason ever dates anyone, darling. We saw each other, while seeing other people. But I will marry him someday." She's deceptively casual. "Old contract between our parents. I just figured you should hear it from me. You seem sweet, but he's going to chew you up and spit you back out when there's nothing left."

I smile back at her, showing all my teeth. "Thanks for letting me know, *darling*."

What a bitch.

Although, it doesn't mean she was necessarily wrong.

# CHAPTER THIRTY-THREE

Tuning out Yuki's words was easier said than done. I've almost convinced myself I've put it behind me by the time I reach my friends. One look at me, and Gabriella asks, "Who do I have to punch?"

Which is hilarious coming from such a sweet-looking cutie.

"No one. I'm good." We've made headway toward the bartender. Olivia orders all our drinks and flashes her ID when Mr. Tall, Dark and Handsome asks her for it.

I'm half expecting him to ask for ours too, but he sweeps our group with one glance and doesn't bother. He probably knows we all have fake IDs if showing them is necessary.

He slides the last of our drinks across the bar at us, when arms wrap around me. I don't have to turn to recognize the distinctive scent.

"Hello. You must be my Nadia's friends." He's

pouring on the charm he uses when he feels like it. Fake as fuck, and but efficient nonetheless.

My friends stare in shock before glaring at me like I committed a cardinal sin.

All right, I might not have mentioned Jason's existence to anyone, because what the hell was I supposed to say? *"Hey, there's a cute guy who likes to torment me."*

"I'm Jason," he introduces himself. "You mind if I kidnap her for a bit?"

I expect my friends to say they very much mind. They're protective as hell, after all. We have each other's backs.

"Absolutely," Gabriella agrees.

"Any time!"

Harper nods wordlessly, basically eye-fucking him.

I turn to him, realizing a little too late that in doing so, I'm facing him while pressed flush against him. "What if I mind, Alden?"

He leans into me, just like Paul did an hour ago. "You don't."

I could knee him in the balls. I could ask Gabriella for help. She's armed with a brand-new glass too.

But he happens to be right, so I just roll my eyes, following him when he tugs my wrist and heads toward the staircase at the back of the bar.

He looks really fucking good in a soft white shirt open at the throat and with jeans low on his hips.

From the sweat glistening on his brow, I'd say he's been dancing.

His outfit isn't that different from our uniform —a shirt and pants—but somehow, it's night and day. I would never guess this guy is a senior in high school if I didn't know him. He looks older, all broad shoulders and lean muscles. Not to mention the sinful way his pants fit him.

Dammit. I hate that I can't look away.

It's a high climb to the second floor, and we proceed in silence at a leisurely pace that allows me to look at the circus girls from higher up and sip my drink.

"This is an epic club," I admit.

The music's a little less loud from this distance —I don't have to shout.

Jason shrugs. "We needed somewhere to chill. Our parents meet at the Heritage building, and we do have a floor we can use over there, but would you party a floor down from your folks?"

I laugh. "Hell, no." Well, my mother, I wouldn't mind that much, but I don't even like my father seeing me in a mini skirt. He doesn't say anything, but the judgement pisses me off.

"Exactly." He grins back at me.

"So, how do you know *of* my mother?" I ask, remembering where we left our text conversation.

He shrugs. "She hangs out at the Heritage sometimes—with my father's generation. She and your... how do you call him again? Uncle?"

My eyebrows hike up an inch. "Yeah?"

He nods. "She has an honorary admission. She's not a member, but she's welcome occasionally. My parents know her well. That makes me think..."

Jason removes his phone from his back pocket and navigates through apps for a few moments. My phone rings in my purse. I take it out, and look.

He's sent me a form, of all things.

It has an H on the letterhead, and like his barcode-slash-invitation card, the background is black with white font.

"An NDA?" I say, scanning the first few words.

He nods. "This is members-only territory—you'll have to sign it before I let you in."

I blink, confused. "And if I don't?"

He shrugs. "I take you back downstairs to your friends, and we'll do this next time, when you feel comfortable enough to sign."

*What the hell?*

"*This*? What is *this*? Why do I have to sign an NDA?"

The corner of his mouth hitches up a little. "I suppose you'll find out after signing."

This guy is seriously frustrating.

I sit on the stairs and read each word, because I'm not about to sign anything before combing every word of it. Jason sits next to me, and starts to twirl my hair around a finger.

I glare at him. "Stop distracting me."

He laughs and leaves me to it.

It looks like a standard NDA—I signed one a couple of months back when going to my uncle's company. It wasn't necessary before I turned eighteen, but for legal reasons, I had to this summer. Not that I ever saw anything super-secret. I only dropped by there occasionally at lunch time to bring Uncle Lucius some sandwiches.

This one threatens to sue me to the tune of a million dollars if I divulge anything going on within the premises—the exception being to report criminal activity. It also adds that the Heritage and its affiliates could retaliate by sharing compromising information about me. My uncle's NDA was stricter, promising criminal charges for opening my trap.

Finally, I sign the document.

"There. Happy?"

"Ecstatic." He gets to his feet and offers me a hand. I let him help me stand, and cross the last few steps heading to the upper floor.

## CHAPTER THIRTY-FOUR

Nothing could have prepared me.

Well, that's a lie. Jason prepared me—as much as he could have before making me sign his document—and so did Yuki, downstairs. I doubt her goal was to make this easier on me, but what she said makes an awful lot of sense once I cross the threshold.

Hell, my *mother* prepared me earlier today.

All the same, I absolutely would never have guessed what I was walking into.

Which makes me sound dumb. After all, haven't I seen Jason with his three friends, fucking the hell out of a girl just a few months back? I suppose I must have erased that from my mind, or assumed it was an isolated incident.

I don't know. I don't know anything. I'm frozen in place, incapable of rational thought or movement.

I'm watching. I can't stop myself. My eyes are greedy, taking in every inch of the place.

The room we walked into is less than half the size of the club downstairs—still large, but more intimate.

I laugh. That's the perfect word for the situation.

Intimate.

Just like downstairs, there are booths along the walls, with luxurious dark leather upholstery. The furniture is roomier—the rows of sofas are something between a bed and a bench. And on most of those benches my schoolmates and a few strangers around our age are fucking.

That's a broad generalization. I see a girl who's just drinking her cosmo with some guy. They're not fucking.

Never mind, he just shoved his hand between her legs. She's widening them.

Cain's head is thrown over the high back of his booth as a woman whose face I can't see blows him. Another girl climbs next to them, whispers in his ear, giggles, and stands over him before lowering herself to his mouth. I don't suppose she's wearing underwear.

It's a veritable orgy. The beat of the music downstairs is echoed here, but at a low volume. I mostly hear moans, screams of pleasure, and begging.

One girl's with five guys. One guy's with three girls. There's a guy fucking another guy, and two girls scissoring each other in the same booth.

"You can run away."

I don't know what to say. I don't know what I think. But I know running away isn't my current instinct. I'm...curious. I have questions.

"There are private rooms on this side." He gestures to a door on the right. "And a dungeon here, for those who like a little more spice with their play." Jason makes a face. "Not my scene."

"What's your scene?" I hear myself ask.

He shrugs. "This. Watching. Being watched." I lift my head and see that he's scrutinizing every one of my expressions. "Sharing," he adds.

*Fuck.*

My eyes return to the proclivities before me. I down the rest of my drink.

Jason laughs. "Let's get you another one of those, yes?"

"Please."

We walk to the bar at the end of the space. That involves getting closer to the crowd, passing through the few couples dancing on the small floor here. There aren't many. They're more interested in fucking. Some of the dancers touch themselves under their clothes.

I focus on the bar, trying to clear my mind.

"You're not running," he notes.

I don't know what to say. "I might later? We'll see when the shock wears off."

"Really?" Jason tilts his head. "Cain told me he saw you last year, when we were in the lockers with whoever it was. You watched for quite a while before leaving, according to him."

My jaw drops. "Cain saw me?"

He shrugs. "He wasn't about to let you know and make you run prematurely. As I said, we like being watched."

Given what I'm seeing right now, it's silly, but I'm still embarrassed.

"There are a lot of legacies here. Are all of you guys..." The bartender interrupts, handing me my new drink, and a glass of Scotch for Jason.

"Not all, no." He drinks a sip. "The Heritage Club started as a gentleman's club, with all the depravity that could entail a few generations ago. It morphed when three of the members married some of the..." He weighs his words. "Female employees."

"Prostitutes. You mean they had prostitutes."

Jason shrugs. "It was the 20s, doll. Between Prohibition and the post-war mess, they were having whatever fun they could. Anyway, they started sharing wives. Other members figured that was a good practice, too. The thing is, when you're raised by swingers, it changes what you consider the norm. You might have seen Mommy and Daddy kiss, while not kissing anyone else? I grew up watching my mom kiss my best friend's dad. That's my norm."

He pauses to gauge my reaction. I honestly don't know what he finds, but it makes him continue.

"The Heritage doesn't hire prostitutes these days. Well, not *many*. The club hires a few escorts from time to time, but they generally work with our grandparents." He wrinkles his nose. "I guess things get less fun at that age, especially when they lose their partners."

I nod, because most of the girls I see are my classmates. They're wealthy, bored, and privileged. The only reason why they would do this...is because they want to.

"Most of the legacy kids end up joining the club. Some don't." He shrugs. "There are a few of us who somehow end up monogamous."

"Somehow," I echo. He says it like it's a rare and incomprehensible choice.

Jason's eyes bore into mine. "Monogamy is the default vision in our society, and everything else is seen as deviant by the masses—but when you're raised in this world? It's like seeing a bunch of vegans never questioning whether they should even try eggs or milk. A lot of those who do try end up liking it. Some remain vegans. Likewise, some omnivores also decide to switch to a more restrictive diet. It's less common, though."

I appreciate the analogy, because it's a lot easier to imagine when I think about food rather than fucking different people in front of an entire room.

"So, you're polyamorous."

"No," he replies immediately, without hesitation. "I'm not romantically interested in various people. Hell, I can't even imagine the effort forming several relationships could take."

He lifts a finger and softly massages a spot

between my eyebrows. I realize I'm frowning, and relax my face. He smiles. "Better."

"So, what then?" I try to stay focused on the subject.

Jason tilts his head to the rest of the room. "I like this. Wild sex. Sharing. Swinging. But at the end of the day, I'd want to go home to one person." His hand moves to my chin, and lifts it. "I want to go home to you, Nadia. I want to fuck you every night, every day. And I want to watch you get fucked occasionally. Potentially while fucking someone else while *you* watch. Never without you." He grimaces, disgusted with himself. "Seriously, it's pathetic. Almost two months and I haven't even been able to get it up for anyone. You messed up my game, big time. I hope you're sorry."

"I'm sorry," I lie.

He shakes his head, usually cold eyes laughing over the rim of his drink.

"Why do you drink Scotch? It's disgusting. Are you an old man in disguise?"

I'm changing the subject to give me time to think, and he lets me.

"Maybe you haven't tried good Scotch."

He offers me his glass. I sniff it and shake my head. "Pass on eau de piss. I love myself too much for that."

Jason laughs out loud. "That's a five-hundred-buck bottle, doll."

"Expensive piss."

At school, he's always been tense whenever I've seen him in public. Now, we're surrounded by four dozen people—admittedly, they're otherwise engaged and not paying us much attention—yet he's relaxed.

*This place? It's Jason's,* Yuki said.

Ugh. Apparently, she'd been right.

Which makes me think... "Yuki let me know you guys were engaged, by the way."

He doesn't seem surprised. Nor does he rush to deny it. "I wouldn't say engaged. When we were like, five, her father asked mine what he'd think about joining our families. It's complex here. With our way of life? Most of us are distant cousins. Cain's Rowan's brother," he tells me. Before I can ask any questions, Jason says, "The Moores and the Aldens haven't crossed that line yet somehow. My dad said sure, so long as one of my sons is amenable."

I nod, like semi-betrothals are totally normal.

Jason is from another world.

"Yuki's hot. When we were growing up, Alexander and I fought over her, actually. Then, it was just me. And I didn't have a reason to not go along with our parents' desires until recently." He holds my gaze. "I told my dad I wanted out weeks ago, Nadia. He's already let the Moores know. Yuki's pissed because she's not used to losing anything, but she doesn't really care. It was business, nothing more."

I can't quite bring myself to believe he'd walk away from an agreement he was happy to follow for years. "Weeks ago," I repeat.

Jason doesn't reply. Instead, he brings his lips to mine and I lose my grip on reality.

## CHAPTER THIRTY-FIVE

His kiss is leisurely at first, like he has all the time in the world. He wraps me in a tender embrace I didn't know him capable of. But I want more. I need more. I'm the one deepening the kiss, *taking*.

Jason moans into my mouth and shifts me on top of him on the bar stool. I'm straddling his hardness, heat pulsing and lighting my skin, my core, my soul on fire.

With a deep inhale, Jason forces himself to stop and leans back.

"I don't want to push you too hard, too fast, Nadia. I threw a bomb at you. Well, several, actually. Do you need time to process all of this?"

Did I? I should, right? That was the sensible thing. The normal thing.

*"If you want to make room for this boy in your life, I want you to have an open mind, all the while paying attention to what you want—what you feel."*

That's what my mom told me. Because she knew where getting involved with Jason would lead. My mother, who attends the Heritage parties. With my uncle.

What the fuck?

I've shelved that information for a while, and I shove it right back where it belongs, at the back of my mind.

"Jason?"

"Yeah?"

"Shut up and kiss me."

He doesn't make me beg. Much.

He does, however, endeavor to drive me completely insane, his mouth sucking along my jawline and neck as his skilled hands run along my thighs, my stomach—over my dress.

"Please, Jason."

He laughs against my throat. "What do you want, doll?"

"You." I need him inside me more than I need my next breath.

Part of me feels like I shouldn't do this here. The bartender's right behind Jason, polishing glasses, not paying us any attention. And behind my back, there are bunches of people fucking.

Another part of me *likes* this. *Wants* this.

He lowers the hem of my neckline over my breasts. I'm not wearing a bra—they're mostly a joke for my B-cup boobs, unless I'm running.

Jason doesn't seem to think they're too small. He takes my nipple in his mouth and sucks on it, caressing my other tit with one hand as the other ventures under my dress along my tights. When he gets to their elastic band, he lowers it and finds the bundle of nerves screaming for attention at the apex of my legs.

I can barely breathe. I can't take it all, and at the same time I need more. So much more.

"About fucking time!"

I can't help glancing over my shoulder. Then I groan. Rowan's standing right behind us, shirtless, the top button of his chinos undone, walking next to a leggy blonde who waves at me. "Hey, new girl."

I'm blushing furiously. "Hi!" My voice is breathless because Jason doesn't stop—not even for a moment. In fact, his fingers curve inside me. He lets go of my nipple only to lick the rest of my breast with the tip of his tongue. Then his mouth moves to my other breast, replacing his hand.

Rowan orders his and his partner's drinks, but his amused gaze stays on us.

Fuck. I think I get wetter. Jason groans when he notices just that.

"I'm Vienna Mayfair," the girl tells me, like I'm not half naked and getting fingered right before her. "I'd heard you landed Alden. Good on you, sister. Don't hesitate to buzz me if you need anything, 'kay?"

She and Rowan get their drinks and leave.

"That was weird."

"A little," Jason says with a laugh. "But you liked it."

I did.

He gets to his feet, holding me under the thighs, and moves us to the closest booth, gently setting me back down on the leather. My small tits are spilling out of my dress, and my skirt is scrunched up to my waist.

Jason rips the crotch of my tights and grins at my polka dot cotton panties—they clash with my short, sexy dress. “I love these,” he announces. “I’d like to see them often.”

Moving the panties aside, he bends down to thrust his head between my legs.

*Oh fuck.*

Jason knows what he’s doing. Like, seriously.

I thought he was a maestro with his hands, but what he does with his mouth, lips, and teeth is out of this world. He teases. He sucks. He licks and blows, all the while fucking me with his fingers, faster, harder.

I hear myself gasp his name in a plea he ignores. Then I’m incapable of forming words, sticking to whimpers and broken moans.

I don’t see the climax coming, but all of a sudden, everything in me burns and tightens, then flows away.

I think I might have died, at least a little.

My next breath surprises me, deep and shaky all at once. I only have a second to contemplate the fact that I am, in fact, alive, before he drags me by the hips to the edge of the bench, and sets both of my ankles over one of his shoulders. I didn't even see him open his fly, but his thick, long, and curved cock is at my entrance, unsheathed.

"Condom. We should have..."

"I'm clean. Are you?"

I nod. Still, "I'm not on birth control."

He wets his lips, his tip teasing my clit. "I'd like to feel you the first time."

He remains at my entrance, eyes on me, waiting for me to protest or assent. I don't do either. I remain silent, incapable of voicing the stupid-ass thought in my head. Who cares what he wants, we should totally wear a condom.

But we're clean and I want to feel him too.

I feel young, stupid, tipsy, and in that moment, immortal. Nothing can touch me.

Except him.

He plunges into me in one deep thrust, filling me so completely. "Fuck. You're so fucking tight, Nadia."

Only because he's so fucking big. His hips move back and slam back home, making me yelp in surprise and delight. And again. And again, faster, deeper. I get hotter, tighter, each of my nerves painfully aware of him. I don't think sex could possibly get any better when he moves my legs again, pushing them back against the seat. He has to climb on top of me to fuck me from above, his cock plunging straight up and down. The new angle is too fucking much. He's hitting a part of me that burns like a furnace each time he moves.

His thumb presses on my clit, then rubs it. "I'm so, so close, doll. You have to come with me."

I cry. I can't form words or thoughts or any sound other than an overwhelmed sob.

Jason's faster, each move bleeding into the next, and my hips move to meet him, my body instinctively knowing just what both of us need. This time, I see the cliff. I see the edge of the precipice.

I fall.

He remains on top of me as his hotness pours inside me just as I clench around him. Both of us are panting hard, his mouth close to mine. He kisses me, dropping on top of me.

I don't know how long we stay there, just breathing. Just *being*.

Then I playfully smack his ridiculously muscular arm. "You came inside me, idiot!"

He chuckles over me. "Was I supposed to do it on your dress? Your face? Let me know for future reference."

"If I ever let you back in my pussy after that."

He snorts. "Please. It's basically my pussy."

The fucking balls on this guy. I wiggle underneath him. "You're crushing me."

"Well, it's not my fault if you like it."

I don't think I've ever seen him so playful. So free.

Now I'm painfully aware of where we are, and the fact that we're most definitely not the only ones thus occupied right now.

"I should check on my friends."

Jason straightens up over me and I sit up, arranging my clothes back where they should be. I doubt I'm presentable. I feel wetness between my legs and sweat all over me. I lost my witch's hat on the floor, and I dread to think what my makeup looks like.

"Naturally," he replies smoothly, though I see his expression change a little. It's resumed some of its coldness now that I've reminded him the real world exists.

# CHAPTER THIRTY-SIX

Jason's the picture of polite gentility when I take him downstairs. He buys my crew a round and gets to know them. He's happy to admit he was a bit of a dick to me—understatement—and when Gabriella threatens him if he does it again, he lets her.

He's also not himself—this is the Jason pretending to be Mercutio in lit class. Not mine.

Before we part ways, he extracts a promise from me to get back to school by Sunday night, and I give it. I usually arrive Monday morning, but I'm happy to see him sooner.

Tonight has opened a door for us. It answered some questions and created a thousand more. I still don't know what I think about his...alternative life, I guess?

I know I want him. For now, that's enough.

I don't know how to speak to Mom that Saturday. I can barely look at her without blushing. She notices, and she does exactly the same.

Before I leave Sunday afternoon, she tells me, "You and I have to talk soon. Not yet, but soon, yes?"

I nod, getting into Hulk.

I'm not sure why Jason was so insistent about getting me to attend his Glass party tonight, but I'm looking forward to seeing him.

I stalked my phone incessantly all weekend, but infuriatingly, I had no message. Dating sucks.

Are we dating? I don't know. Probably not. He's always calculated, direct. He would have clearly asked me out if he meant to.

Back at school, I take a shower, because my hair's a lot easier to tame when it's wet.

Unless I'm in a rush, I like to linger under the water, and I do just that, my mind drifting back to Friday night, like it has all weekend. I'm smiling when a piercing alarm blasts through the dorm. I groan. The last thing I need is a fire drill right now, while I'm wearing nothing.

I dry myself as fast as I can and am putting the jeans and T-shirt I was wearing back on when I notice the smoke.

It's coming from all corners of my door, swirling inside the small bathroom.

I grab the door handle and scream in pain. The burning hot metal scorched layers of skin right off my palm.

Hands trembling, I grab a towel and use it to

lower the handle, opening the door slowly, bent down, keeping low to the floor.

My room's on fire.

I don't mean there's a small, containable fire inside my room.

Everything, the bed, the curtains, the floor, my easel, is engulfed in bright flames and smoke.

I don't have anywhere to go but into the flames. Crawling low, as fast as I can, I cross the room to get out, using the towel in order to touch the handle.

I turn it, but nothing happens.

My door is locked, and the key isn't in its hole.

That makes no sense. I don't even use the lock now that I've bought my second inner lock, but the second system is open.

Someone locked me in here.

I know I have a spare key at the bottom of my school bag, but even if I knew exactly where I'd put it down, it wouldn't help—everything is burning.

My eyes hurt. My head is spinning. My throat's dry and hoarse. "Help!"

I scream, scream, and scream some more, desperately thumping my fist on the door.

No one answers.

There's nothing but darkness.

I wake to blinding white everything. Bed, walls, floors. I first think I might be dead and in something akin to paradise. But I couldn't be dead *and* in this much pain.

Everything aches, like I've done a marathon without training. What truly hurts are my hands, feet, and throat.

Trying to move, I feel something restraining my movement. I glance down and see a tube coming out of me.

I start to panic. What's going on?

"Hey. You're awake."

Jason.

My heart beats a little slower, calming down.

He's seated next to me, looking as rumpled as he's ever looked—like he might have sat there for a long time.

"I'm going to call the nurse, okay?" He holds up a button.

I can't reply, because there's a tube down my throat.

I start to cry.

"Hey, hey. You're okay. Everything's going to be fine. You hear me?"

I do, but I can't believe him.

I was locked in a room set ablaze. On purpose. Someone wanted me dead. How could I ever be okay again? The fear, the recollection of the utter certainty of my impending death is too much.

A male nurse in blue scrubs enters the room. "Ms. Reyes! I'm Jonathan. I've been taking care of you for the last few hours. I'm glad you've come through."

He calmly explains to me that the tube is helping get some air into my lungs—I inhaled too much smoke. He checks the machines I'm plugged in to alongside an IV I hadn't even noticed and tells me he can remove them now.

Please, please, please, my eyes say, and he must have understood, because he does it.

My throat hurts. I look down at my bandaged hand.

"You were very lucky your friend here came to check on you," the nurse says, gesturing to Jason.

I'm crying again.

"The door. It was locked. How..."

"I broke it down. You were right behind it, so it hit your head," he adds apologetically.

The sobbing coming out of me is uncontrollable. I'm alive. He saved me. He came to check on me.

I fall asleep.

---

Jason's sleeping the next time I come to. My bladder is making itself known. I look at the IV in my arm, then grab the liquid pouch it's attached to, before rushing to the toilet in my hospital room.

Things are clearer now. My nerves are less frayed. I can think more or less clearly.

Someone did try to kill me, and there could be only one reason why they would.

There's nothing special about me. I don't have tons of money, like most of my peers. I don't have true enemies—no one who could have an actual reason to want me dead.

Except for the boy next to me.

Being with Jason is a rush like nothing else. Getting lost in the flow of art doesn't compare. He's the sweetest poison, everything that should make me run a mile drawing me in instead.

I think back to the poor cat killed just this Monday because of Jason making me a target. One week later, it could have been me.

There's a new player in the game Jason and I began, and they have their own set of rules.

If I stay with him, I could be the next corpse he buries.

I can't do this. To him or to me.

## YEARS AGO

### Jace

The boy who looked like me rested against velvet and wood, unmoving, as if asleep. For the first time in our eight years, Alexander seemed smaller than me. I suppose it wasn't impossible that I might have gained half an inch or so on him. My twin was younger than I was now, because he'd spent the last few days dead.

He shouldn't have been dead. Death was for the old, and the sick, and anyone who wasn't Alexander Alden. My brother. My reflection. My everything.

He was dead, and I should have been too.

*What would it be like to be inside the coffin? Cold, I suppose, though I don't think corpses feel cold. I'll have to ask Father. I don't think Mother would appreciate this line of questioning.*

For a moment, as I stared at him, I imagined myself in his place.

It could have been me. It *should* have been me.

All of these people would have been here because of me, if it hadn't been for sheer luck. I would be the one unable to move or play or sing. But I wouldn't sing again. There was blood on my fingers, blood I couldn't wipe off if I wanted to, and I didn't. Killers didn't get to sing. Killers didn't get to play. Killers didn't get to *feel*. Besides, Alex wasn't here to listen. What was the point?

What was the point in anything?

My mother was weeping again. She hadn't stopped, not in three days. She stood behind me while my father kept a steady hand on both of our shoulders. He might have wanted to reassure me, or keep me where he could see me, now that I was his only heir. His hand made me feel as if I was trapped there, forever under his control.

I shivered. I wasn't sure if the church was cold or if I was. There had been an emptiness inside of me since the police returned with Alex's body. A numbness that I doubted would ever leave. Cold and numb, just like the corpse that looked like me.

I remembered asking Mother years before what happened after we died, and she told me we became memories in the hearts of those who loved us. Alex didn't look like a memory. Nor did the man I killed in retaliation for my brother's death.

That man had looked like meat after I'd pulled the trigger. Alex? He was like a wax doll, not quite real.

Eventually, my father shuffled us along to our seats, and shortly after that, the wake started. The procession moved from the church to the cemetery, and I moved along with it.

Cold and numb.

So many people talked—to me, to Father and Mother. Too many of them offered apologies. Why would they? They had nothing to do with Alex's death. I hated empty words more than I hated just about anything. The more they talked, the number I felt. I could hardly make out the throng of bodies, the word vomit coming out of their mouths, lost in my own head, in the memories my mother had promised. All I could hear were my brother's screams.

*Go!*

He'd wanted me to run and get help. To come back for him, to save him.

By the time I'd made it back, he was a corpse.

I'd been too slow. I'd gotten lost in the woods. If I'd been faster, stronger, smarter, Alex would be at football camp and I, practicing with Mrs. Vers.

My stomach twisted into knots, and I thought I might be sick. Father wouldn't approve. Even standing to walk away to the bathroom wouldn't be looked at kindly, so I remained there and swallowed down the bile, lest I make a scene.

I knew how to hold myself in public. I was an Alden. The only Alden left.

Why me? Alex was the heir. The firstborn. The one who was good with numbers and dates, and at sports, too.

No longer.

My twin was dead.

That one thought was all I could focus on. His screams grew louder in my mind.

*Go! Jace, Go! Run!*

I had run, and he wasn't here anymore.

Neither of us had ever truly been alone, even when he was playing football and I stayed home. I'd always felt him. When he broke his arm the year before, I could tell something was wrong before we got the call. I could always tell when he was about to come back. We were one.

We had been one.

I could be with him, though. I *could* join him. There was a way for us to be reunited. I knew where Father kept the gun. There was a lock, but he'd never been imaginative with passwords. Our birthday? Mother's? Their wedding anniversary? If I got to the gun, I could use it again, just like I had the previous night. I could—

I was abruptly yanked out of my own head when a pair of arms enveloped me. Someone was hugging me. Hard.

We weren't huggers in my family. Not there, in public. Mother did hug me sometimes, but I could tell this wasn't her. It felt different. Smaller, but also stronger. My eyes flew open. I wasn't even sure when I'd closed them.

A girl. I was being hugged by a girl.

I didn't know many girls. I was homeschooled. Father's friends had a few children around my age, but the girls stuck to themselves. Dark wavy hair covered my shoulder. That was all I could see of her because her head was buried against my chest.

I could smell her, though. She was like the sea, like summer and candy.

I choked on a sob. I hadn't cried in three days. Father was proud of me for it; he told me that men don't show weakness. But the sob? I couldn't help it. She forced it out of me. I wanted to lash out at her for making me show weakness right in front of my brother's casket, but instead, I hugged her back, and lowered my face onto her shoulder so no one could see my eyes. I wasn't crying. I wasn't capable of it, though she made me feel as though I almost could. But my eyes watered all the same.

"Nadia, darling, we should go."

I registered the soft voice I didn't recognize, but I ignored it. Nadia. Her name was Nadia. But she wasn't going anywhere.

She was *mine*.

"Nadia..."

"In a minute," the girl replied. Her voice was a song, and I memorized each intonation, each chord.

She tightened her hold on me as I blinked my unshed tears away. Then finally, the girl drew back and stared up at me with eyes that couldn't decide if they were brown or green.

She looked terribly sad. Her eyes were red with tears. I didn't like it. I managed a smile for her. "It'll be all right."

Strange that I was the one saying those words to her.

Stranger yet, I believed them.

Everything would be fine. I would survive. I would *thrive*. I was Jason Alden, and from that day on, I would have to live for Alexander Alden, too. I'd accomplish everything he'd wanted to achieve.

She smiled and moved away from me, tugged back by a pretty lady dressed all in black like my mother. The woman looked vaguely familiar. I must have seen her at an event.

The girl was leaving with three adults—two men and the pretty lady. Trailing her steps, I cleared my throat, pulling at my father's sleeve, though he was talking to the CEO of one of the companies he owned.

"Yes?" Charles Alden's voice was cool and commanding, even with a single word.

"Who is that?" I nodded toward her, not wanting to point. My mother had impressed on my brother and I that pointing was rude.

Father's jaw tightened as he followed my gaze. I observed him closely. I could tell. He knew her—or at least, the adults in her company. Why would they be here otherwise? After a long moment, he said, "No one."

I frowned.

She was someone to me.

She was the cold crash of waves against a cliff. She was summer to my dark, cold, and numb mind.

*Nadia*.

I stared at the girl as she was pulled away by her

mother. She looked back at me, and I did my best to memorize everything about her.

I didn't think I would ever forget the dark eyes filled with tears that I couldn't dare shed.

Turned out, I did.

For a while.

The End

Did you enjoy *I Fucking Dare You*? Emm writes several books under three pen names. If you'd like her to prioritize this world, don't hesitate to let her know by leaving a review.

The second and last book about Jason and Nadia, *Spin The Damn Bottle,* is available for preorder.

Catch up with Emm in her facebook group here for news and offers <3

Milton Keynes UK
Ingram Content Group UK Ltd.
UKHW031858061224
452277UK00017B/196/J

9 781839 840579